Johnathan,
Daniel Parsons

Justice

S. J. McDonald

Justice

By S. J. McDonald

This book was first published in Great Britain in paperback during August 2024.

The moral right of S. J. McDonald is to be identified as the author of this work and has been asserted by her in accordance with the Copyright, Designs and Patents Act of 1988.

All rights are reserved and no part of this book may be reproduced or utilized in any format, or by any means, electronic or mechanical, including photocopying, recording or by any information storage or retrieval system, without prior permission in writing from the publishers - Coast & Country/Ads2life. ads2life@btinternet.com

All rights reserved.

ISBN: 979-8336096613

Copyright © August 2024 S. J. McDonald

This work is fictional. The names, characters, businesses, organisations, places, locales, incidents and events depicted are either resultant of the author's imagination or used completely in a fictitious manner.

Any similarity to any actual person, alive or dead or any specific events or incidents are purely coincidental.

Dedicated to everyone who feels the darkness, but continues to search for the light.

Acknowledgments

For everyone who I have loved and received love from, they will live forever in my heart.

Enormous thanks goes to my small team of willing and dedicated proof readers, namely Marie Digner, Angela Smith and Anne Williams. You ladies have been a great help and a constant source of encouragement, for which I am eternally grateful. Additional thanks goes to fellow author Steve Naylor for his time, advice and support. The insights into his extensive career at the very highest levels of policing have been invaluable.

And finally, special recognition for all the support received with this and every endeavour goes to my wonderful husband Ian, without whom I would achieve nothing.

About the Author

Sarah McDonald lives in the North West of England with her childhood sweetheart and husband of many years, Ian. Where they are surrounded by their unconventional and extremely loving family.

She has had a varied and productive career in the NHS spanning a total of 36 years, achieving senior roles in both nursing and management. As an avid reader herself, she has always loved books and in particular crime fiction. So following retirement, it seemed a logical step for her to call upon her vast experiences in the creation of exciting new books for others to enjoy.

Published in 2024, Justice; is her first book, in a series of novels, that feature the straight talking Yorkshire born and raised, Manchester based Detective Inspector Thomas Marsden.

Sarah took inspiration for the main character and focus of her books from a number of sources close to her heart and as such she feels a real connection to the well-meaning, at times flawed, 'Tommy'.

Contents

Preface 1

Part 1.. 7

Chapter 1... 9

Chapter 2... 17

Chapter 3... 25

Chapter 4... 31

Chapter 5... 34

Chapter 6... 47

Chapter 7... 59

Chapter 8... 67

Chapter 9... 80

Chapter 10... 84

Chapter 11... 90

Chapter 12... 101

Chapter 13... 109

Chapter 14... 117

Chapter 15... 124

Chapter 16... 129

Chapter 17	136
Chapter 18	140
Chapter 19	149
Chapter 20	153
Chapter 21	159
Chapter 22	169
Chapter 23	173
Chapter 24	178
Chapter 25	185
Chapter 26	190
Chapter 27	201
Chapter 28	209
Chapter 29	215
Chapter 30	223
Chapter 31	226
Chapter 32	232
Chapter 33	240
Chapter 34	244
Part 2	249
Chapter 35	251
Chapter 36	258

Chapter 37	274
Chapter 38	282
Chapter 39	289
Chapter 40	294
Chapter 41	304
Chapter 42	315
Chapter 43	322
Chapter 44	333
Chapter 45	336
Chapter 46	338
Chapter 47	347
Chapter 48	350
Chapter 49	356
Chapter 50	367
Chapter 51	376
Chapter 52	381
Chapter 53	387
Chapter 54	392
Chapter 55	406
Epilogue	409

Suicide is a permanent solution to a temporary problem

Phil Donahue - American media personality

Preface

It was a beautiful crisp spring day, the sort of day that made your skin feel cold and your soul warm at the same time. The sky was a clear, almost a transparent pale blue; the sun doing its damnedest to brighten the wretched scene. He was suddenly aware of a flock of birds overhead and hushed voices in the distance.

He stood silently, for some reason mesmerised by how green the grass seemed to be in contrast to the bright young daffodils and the few remaining snowdrops and crocuses. He looked down and noticed that droplets of the morning dew were gathering on his shoes, his highly polished, super black shoes, 'you can tell a lot about a man by his shoes' she had always professed. Was that true he wondered now, was it important; was anything really important anymore?

He was numb, stunned, perhaps shocked. Of course he knew this day would come; having feared it since she was diagnosed and he had later been broken when the doctor first explained that despite initial surgery and three rounds of chemotherapy 'they were now looking at end of life care' in conclusion he had said how sorry he was as he explained 'there was no more to be done'.

He was so angry as he had played the scenario over and over in his head 'They! - They were now looking at end of life care!' it seemed as if the doctor thought he was somehow involved, that it affected him, but he wasn't involved, wasn't affected, he could never really understand the enormity of the situation. The love he and Cathy shared was a one off; unique, so incredibly special that he had felt that his life had also ended when she said her final goodbye.

She had always been his better half, and even in her final days she had never complained, only ever being practical, making sure he would be okay when she had gone. A small smile flashed momentarily on his lips, actively battling his obvious misery and exhaustion, as he remembered banal conversations about household bills and address books complete with lists of essential birthdays and anniversaries he mustn't forget.

Their love had been rare, matchless and he was constantly aware of how friends and colleagues had envied them both throughout the years, often stating how lucky they were to have found one another.

He had had an unconventional childhood, he had not wanted for much; raised by his grandparents he had been surrounded by love. Like so many he had used his early experiences as a template for the future. He had always wanted a loving home, a supportive partner and from the moment he met her he knew that Cathy was all he had ever wanted and so much more. She was the love of his life, his one and only, she was special and what they shared was irreplaceable.

He pictured her now, her sun kissed hair blowing in the gentle breeze and her gorgeous eyes shining as she smiled. She was so unbelievably beautiful inside and out and as he thought of her he became aware that an insurmountable anger was being cultivated yet again somewhere deep within his stomach, the now familiar crushing waves of grief engulfing him once more.

In the last few weeks his GP had provided him with tablets he hadn't taken, whilst neighbours had cooked casseroles he hadn't eaten and friends and colleagues seemed to have an endless supply of advice he didn't want and certainly never asked for. He knew they all meant well but the platitudes were close to driving him mad. He tried to focus on the here and now, knowing he had to just get through this dreadful day, but as he looked skywards he thought to himself that if one more person asked him how he was feeling he really wouldn't be responsible for his actions.

"How are you Tommy?" He was suddenly brought back to the present and the chilly churchyard, the sun had been temporarily defeated once more, having disappeared behind some angry darkened clouds, and it seemed perfect symbolism of the occasion.

"I'm fine thanks Ish." He found himself saying and despite himself he couldn't help cracking a wry smile at the handsome, young man who stood in front of him, as he considered the comedy timing of their interaction.

They stood in silence and after a lengthy pause he explained to his trusty Sergeant that what he wanted was to get back to work as soon as possible, that he needed some semblance of normality back. He had always had a need to be doing something useful, and despite the long hours and the frustration he often felt at the increasing number of tasks that frequently got in the way of his work, he still cherished being a good old fashioned copper, enjoying the comfort and certainty derived from playing his part in delivering straight forward justice.

He realised that now was as good a time as any to explain to his friend that he had already spoken to the Chief and that he would be back in the driving seat the following week.

Part 1.

Chapter 1

She took the opportunity to quickly glance at her watch whilst no one was looking; ten past three on a Friday afternoon, her heart sank. She would be lucky if she was home before midnight at this rate. She loved her job and knew only too well that 'to get ahead you had to play the game', as her old Ward Sister Maggie used to frequently say and although the value of her mentors advice fluctuated greatly at times, there was no questioning her wisdom when it came to the secret of success: the three P's. Sandy had lost count of how many times she had said that in meetings you always needed to pay attention, push yourself forward and participate. But she would much rather be with the patients doing the job than talking about it.

She took a moment to consider those assembled in the boardroom, the great and the good, all jockeying for position, trying to curry favour with the formidable Caroline Philips, the current Senior Nursing Officer, who posed a very striking figure in her freshly starched burgundy uniform. Sandy tried to remember if she had ever seen her in her uniform outside of these monthly meetings where the agenda always seemed to be the same.

In general she couldn't complain, she had climbed through the ranks quickly, being recognised as a grafter rather than a kiss ass and if truth be known she had no real concerns for her next promotion, as she was on an extremely strong career trajectory, held in high esteem throughout the hospital, seen as a doer by those she managed and a team player who got results by the upper echelons.

As Caroline was discussing the usual subject of budget cuts and doing more for less, Sandy became aware of the dust particles that seemed to be twinkling in a shaft of light from one of the large arch shaped windows of the ancient boardroom, their energetic dancing against the dark panelled walls seemed incongruous, too lively for the stale, musty environment. 'How much bloody

Justice

longer must we sit through this?' she was wondering to herself. She was desperate to leave and start providing some of the much sought after value for money when the thoughts in her head were suddenly interrupted by the piercing screech of the bleep clipped into the inside top pocket of her uniform informing her that she was required elsewhere. She quickly moved to the end of the board room, accessing the only land line in the vicinity and as quietly as possible rang the familiar four numbers on display.

Once the call was answered she identified herself as Sister McKenzie, explaining that someone had bleeped the Senior Nurse on Call. Just a couple of minutes later she silently mouthed her apologies to Caroline, who was now discussing how best the group could make staff feel supported. As she left she couldn't help smiling to herself, as she was thinking that the answer may well be as simple as fewer meetings about support and leadership and more actual support and leadership.

S. J. McDonald

In a way she was relieved to have been summoned by the A&E department, being on call for the entire weekend meant that most of her activity would involve being in and around the Accident and Emergency Department and as such she liked to get a feel for what was going on, which staff were around and what issues they had or were anticipating as soon as was practicable.

As she walked through the corridors there were a number of smiles and head nods, as she acknowledged several staff and patients alike. Despite its size the NHS seemed to be a relatively small place to work at times and inside a busy general hospital like this one almost everyone knew one another and on the 'shop floor' there was a genuine feeling of camaraderie.

On the phone she had been asked to attend the department and advised that a police officer was wanting to speak to her, this wasn't unusual, there was frequently a police presence in and around the urgent care service and as the senior nurse it would be her job

Justice

to assist as required with any number of scenarios, from patients who had taken ill whilst in police custody who needed to be kept secure whilst cared for, to the procedural collection and storage of potential evidence of a crime.

The department was usually busy and to the untrained eye appeared to be chaotic, but she knew that in reality it functioned like a well-oiled machine for the most part and she was proud of the service the staff provided for the local community.

As she approached she could see that the waiting room was not as full as she would have expected, but then again it was a little early for the usual weekend nonsense to have commenced. She spotted the Director of Operations talking with a very attractive uniformed officer who seemed to be hanging on his every word, 'bloody hell what's the occasion?' she silently whispered to herself, this could not be good, it was a rare occasion that he ever left his office, unless there was a press statement to give of course, oh there was no question about it he loved the cameras; but she knew only too well for the majority of his working week he avoided the A&E department like the plague and when his attendance was necessary he had never been known to have got his hands dirty. She wondered now if they had a high profile patient in the department or perhaps a major incident was unfolding somewhere.

She had already resigned herself to a very long shift, that's just how it was, and she really hoped that John would resist the temptation of calling Dominoes for pizza and instead cook some proper food for the kids when he got in from work, she also prayed that it wouldn't be that rubbery chicken in that non-descript sauce he seemed to favour, that was waiting for her in the fridge when she finally got home.

She was quickly ushered into the relative's room, which was a lightly decorated, chintzy affair with soft pink furnishings and comfy chairs, which the staff frequently used for short meetings when all the offices were being used and there were no treatment rooms available in

Justice

which to hold a private conversation. Sandy really disliked the room and given its primary purpose found it to be a sad and cold place.

On entering she was greeted by a large, grey haired man in an ill-fitting dark blue suit, he looked to be in the his late forties or early fifties, but she could be way off, she always thought it was difficult to accurately age a certain type of man. His voice was warm, strong and confident as he identified himself as Detective Inspector Thomas Marsden and he introduced his colleague as Detective Sergeant Ishan Patel, she instantly noticed the younger man was very smartly dressed and had kind dark eyes and a warm smile. Also in the cramped room was a middle aged, dark haired woman, wearing a very off putting salmon coloured skirt and jacket with a cream pussy bow blouse, the detective advised that she was a hospital administrator and as they all sat down Sandy noticed with some disdain that the woman, whose name she had instantly forgotten had bare legs, which she considered to be very unprofessional.

The next few minutes were a blur, the detective was explaining that the body of a young girl had been found, but for some reason she couldn't understand what was being said to her. She heard herself repeatedly saying "No" the tide of blood pulsating in her ears was deafening, drowning out the sound of the voices around her. It felt like the earth had moved, slipped from its axis and like so many others that had been in this god forsaken room before her, she knew her life would never be the same again. Annabel, beautiful, clever, sassy, cheeky, Annabel. Her lovely little Annie was dead.

Chapter 2

Monday morning could not have come soon enough for Tommy, as the only D.I. in the patch, on call since Friday; he had dealt with two sexual assaults, one case of grievous bodily harm with a weapon, namely a garden spade and two suicides. He had also been consulted on a number of minor crimes and infringements and a total of three elderly unexplained deaths, with all three cases appearing to have no suspicious circumstances whatsoever, but nevertheless adding to the mountain of paperwork currently piled high on his desk.

He had been in the office for most of the weekend and as such he was currently looking a little dishevelled and feeling quite jaded, he had decided he would stick around until about ten o'clock, before heading home for a much needed shower and some rest.

Obviously, the sexual assaults had been passed to the dedicated team immediately following his initial investigations and he was pleased that he had already managed to completed the necessary paperwork for each, thus these incidents were no longer his direct concern and barring the unlikely event he was ever called to court as the original senior investigating officer on scene, his role here was complete.

He would farm out the suicides and the GBH to members of his team as they arrived and he would save the follow up on the three unexplained deaths for Carl Slater, whose attitude and tardiness had been grating on his last nerve for a while now. Tommy often wondered how much policing time was wasted on the unexplained deaths of people over the age of eighty and had frequently raised the question with the powers that be of just how unexplained or unexpected these deaths really could be.

He was pulling the weekend files together when he heard the external doors to the office open and seconds later, as could be predicted, the internal door burst open as Claire Johnson, was first to arrive.

Justice

"Busy weekend Boss?" she had worked with him for a little over two years now and always seemed to be happy about something, his grandmother would have described her as having a 'sunny disposition'. He really liked her, not just as a colleague but as a person, although this morning he considered for a moment that her usual singsong voice was perhaps a little too much for his poor, sleep deprived brain.

"As usual it was a joy from beginning to end." He mumbled flashing her a broad smile.

"What do we have then?" She was as keen as ever to get going.

"Bloody hell Claire; give me a minute will you?" He chuckled. He knew that, in part at least, her enthusiasm was driven by the desire to compete and do well in what still remained a male dominated service, with few women reaching the highest of ranks, however, he personally had high hopes for Claire and he wanted to not only nurture her natural instincts and abilities for the job, but also to build her confidence and self-belief, she was a good copper and a massive asset to the team.

"Couple of sex crimes, already passed over, a woman tried to knock some sense into her old man with a shovel and a couple of apparent suicides, ones a kid, plus the usual on call dross."

"Oh, a kid, that's rough." he noticed her tone was not quite so chipper all of a sudden.

"Yeah, both hangings" he said "thirty nine year old male and a fourteen year old girl."

They were both quiet for a moment. Despite national and local prevention and awareness campaigns and increased resources being poured into so called talking therapies, they both knew that sadly, cases of suicide were on the increase across the UK.

Claire's voice was little more than a whisper when she said "Let's hope this isn't the start of some internet fuelled crap."

Justice

"Yeah. Let's hope not." Tommy replied.

They were both aware of how rare it was for any woman, let alone a young girl to end her life in this way and the very thought that this could be part of some new trend was terrifying.

After a minute Tommy continued "...oh I almost forgot we have three of the usual, easily explained, 'unexplained' elderly deaths and all that they entail too."

"Jesus wept! You have been busy. So what's the plan?" She asked retreating back behind the safety shield of business as usual.

"We can divvy up the new cases once everyone gets in, and then I'm going home to freshen up and having a kip."

She smiled as she was walking towards the small office kitchen that they shared with two other teams, lightening the mood she shouted over her shoulder that she hadn't wanted to mention the smell. Tommy replied laughingly that she had better watch it or she would find herself leading the investigations into the elderly deaths.

With the exception of the ever elusive Carl Slater and Ishan Patel, who had gone home for some well-earned sleep following a hectic weekend, and was due back at 2pm, the team were at their desks by 9am and ready for the morning brief.

Tommy gave the team a rundown of the weekend and received updates on a number of on-going cases. Taking into account the current workloads it was agreed that Tommy and Ishan would retain oversight of both suicides, whilst Claire would partner with Tim Jackson, on working up the GBH case. Tim was an extremely capable PC, temporarily working alongside the Criminal Investigations Department. He was on loan to the CID team as part of a nation-wide initiative aimed at up-skilling the average officer on the beat; when in reality everyone knew that to be selected for inclusion into this

Justice

or any other national scheme you needed to be anything but average. Tommy was already wondering how well these two would work together, when Claire was quick to point out that officers Johnson and Jackson sounded like a comedy double act, he made a quick mental note to keep an eye on the situation, checking that their pairing was not considered too much for mere mortals to handle. Just as he was considering the potential down side to having two positive, enthusiastic and effective staff working together Sergeant Slater finally arrived.

"Carl, good of you to call in."

"Morning Boss, sorry I'm late I was following up on something." Tommy hated his laziness and his attitude almost as much as he hated the fact that Carl was frequently 'following up on something!' He felt his jaw clench and realised he was grinding his back teeth again, a constant pet hate of his dentist.

"No problem Carl," he said, "we have three unexplained elder deaths we need to get closed off as soon as possible, so if you have a minute I can go through the paperwork with you," he looked around at the whole team now and stated "right guys let's get to it!"

Thirty minutes later he was out the door, hoping for a quick shower and a long sleep, whilst consciously trying not to let Slater ruin his day or affect his long term dental health.

Chapter 3

Sandy just couldn't seem to understand what had happened, why her happy-go-lucky fourteen year old daughter had killed herself and in such a terribly brutal way. She was her mother, a nurse, surely she would have known if something was bothering Annabel. Obviously teenage years could be difficult, she knew that, and life was so much more complicated now than when she was a girl, but she had always encouraged the girls to talk to her about anything and she thought that they felt comfortable discussing any issues that were troubling them. Annie's death was making her analyse every aspect of her relationship with her children, questioning herself as a parent. Had she done something to cause this? Could she have prevented it? Her mind was in state of constant unrest; she was emotionally drained and physically exhausted.

She took a large cleansing breath before she started again to review every aspect of her parenting, had she been too hard, too soft, or unapproachable? Had she smothered the girls, been over protective? Or was she absent too much, especially when they were younger? She knew the formative years of childhood were immensely important and her job required her to be away from the girls for long periods at a time. She also recognised now, on reflection, that when she was physically present, that she was frequently preoccupied by the things she encountered in the execution of her work. Who wouldn't be affected by the things she saw and did? She took another long breath and as she slowly exhaled she had to consider was she just making excuses for herself? Had she simply failed?

Her mind was in turmoil which was all very alien to her; she was normally a calm, calculated, decisive person, who always knew what she thought and what to do. She hated not being in control of any situation. She continued to torture herself over and over again until

Justice

John appeared in the doorway; he looked every bit as devastated as she felt.

He joined her at the kitchen sink and they both looked out onto the garden, it had been a place of beauty, peace and tranquillity for them for so long, but now it was tainted, ugly, a constant reminder of what their little girl had done. She was plagued by her never ending thoughts about what she must have felt and how they had let her down.

Once she had eventually grasped what the police officers were telling her, Sandy had been escorted from the relative's room outside to an awaiting car. She had wordlessly handed the on call bleep to the Director of Operations, barely conscious of the abnormal quietness surrounding her or the curious eyes following her every move. She had been driven by the woman in the salmon coloured suit from the hospital to a neighbour's house in a blur. The woman must have spoken, must have tried to console her, but she remembered nothing of the journey or what was said. She had not gone home until

Annie's body was removed, this was John's decision and she appreciated the fact that he didn't want her to have that lasting image of their youngest daughter hanging from the oak tree at the end of their previously beautiful garden. But she was also being totally irrational, despising him now for keeping their baby to himself.

Their older daughter, Kristy, was inconsolable, unable to speak without sobbing she refused to be comforted in any way by either of her parents. In fact since Friday evening she had said very little and had hardly moved out of her bedroom. There was a dark shroud of hopelessness engulfing their once happy home and the level of disbelief was tangible.

On Saturday afternoon they had been required to attend the local hospital to formally identify Annabel's body. They were met by Sergeant Patel, the younger of the two officers she had previously met; he had spoken softly and had escorted John and her to the mortuary.

Justice

He had explained that Annabel would be in a separate room. That they couldn't touch her, but they would be able to see her through a window for as long as they wanted. She remembered thinking he was a kind person and she felt a degree of sympathy for him having to deal with such a terrible situation. Once the curtain on the small viewing window was finally opened she was surprised to realise that she felt nothing but emptiness. John was distraught and openly sobbed, but she had no desire to touch or be closer to her daughter. This cold, colourless, lifeless thing before her was not her baby, not her Annie. She had very quickly made eye contact with the policeman and nodded slightly a couple of times before saying "Yes. This is our daughter." With the formalities addressed she had assisted her shattered husband from the department.

Outside she had been handed a clear plastic envelope with a white sticky label on the front that aptly read 'Information for the bereaved'. Sandy had said something stupid like "Well, that's bang on the money" as she stared down at the package whist the officer had once again said he was sorry for their loss.

Johns voice returned her to the here and now "Would you like something to eat or some tea maybe?" his voice was quiet, empty, so different to her now, everything was different now. She wanted to scream that the only thing she wanted was her daughter back, but she didn't have the energy to deal with him if he didn't understand that she didn't want anything, but that which she had so cruelly lost. She wanted to close her eyes and when she opened them for this to have all been a terrible dream, a nightmare, not real, some sort of big mistake.

She suddenly rested her head against his chest and continued to cry, feeling she may never stop.

Chapter 4

Tommy had stood under the shower for a long time, the water so hot that it had gone beyond warming and relaxing his muscles, leaving his skin red, blotchy and sensitive. He had fallen into bed exhausted and yet he had been unable to sleep.

He looked across at the small bottle of tablets the doctor had prescribed for him shortly after Cathy had died. He knew that they may help, but he also knew that he would be unable to work if he took them; he also knew that if he took one he may take them all.

Work was his salvation, his purpose, that's why he had returned to work just one week after her funeral. He needed focus, he had always been that way, even as a child he had an enquiring mind, he needed to know how things worked, how they fitted together and why.

He had been raised by his grandparents for the most part, his father drinking excessively once his mother had died. But his childhood, far from traditional was nevertheless a happy time for him. His grandfather had been an engineer as a younger man and he and Tommy had spent hours on end in his little workshop tinkering with all sorts of gadgets and repairing 'odds and sods' as they called them.

His grandmother had been a formidable woman who always managed to ensure he had a warm home, clean clothes and a full belly despite any hardships they may have endured. He smiled as he thought about the first time he had taken Cathy to Yorkshire to introduce them. She had been so different to any other girl he had previously known, softly spoken and in a lot of ways quite traditional, he had been nervous of what she may have thought of their little cottage in Sheffield, but he needn't have worried, she wasn't materialistic and always saw beyond the superficial. After a lovely afternoon tea his grandfather had simply smiled at his grandmother and pronounced "She'll do!" and he knew at that moment she would be his wife, his one true love.

Justice

He could picture her now with her beautiful sun kissed hair and her hazel eyes that sometimes seemed to have sparkles of green in them. Tommy closed his eyes and slept.

Chapter 5

Tommy was precariously perched on a grubby blue office chair that had clearly seen better days, it offered practically no comfort or lumbar support and one of the five base wheels, original intended to glide effortlessly across the chequerboard blue and grey carpet tiles, seemed to be continually jammed, hence it was always available and never did anything to improve his mood. He didn't bother to lift his head from the file he was reading as he addressed the room.

"Slater let's start with you, shall we." It was a statement more than a question.

"Sir" was the succinct reply received from the right hand side of the open plan office.

Making eye contact now he asked "Where are we with the three unexplained deaths?" It was Tuesday morning and for once the errant sergeant was actually at his desk

Justice

at the start of proceedings. Carl adjusted his tie and began to enlighten the team on his findings thus far. "We have successfully identified all three of the deceased consisting of two males and one female as Malcolm Miller, Howard Scholes and Delilah Jones." Tommy was unimpressed thus far, as in his opinion a small child could have secured positive ID's on the three, given that they were all found in their own homes. He resisted the temptation to roll his eyes or jolly his colleague along. Carl continued whilst he had the floor "The post-mortems on all three had been undertaken and Doctor Fogerty has conclusively ruled that there were no suspicious circumstances in any of the deaths," Carl further explained "the bodies of Mr Malcolm Miller and Mrs Delilah Jones have now been made available to their families and the paperwork is completed; however, the next of kin in the matter of Howard Scholes has yet to be identified. It appears that the unfortunate Mr Scholes may have been deceased for up to two weeks before the smell eventually alerted a none too observant neighbour to the situation."

Tommy smiled momentarily as he recalled that the original PC attending the scene had described it as a 'bit funky' at the time. He looked over at Carl who was now ending his update with the all too familiar sentence. "...and I will therefore need to do some follow up on this before the third case can be concluded."

Tommy who couldn't help but wonder if Slater had ever just finished a piece of work in one go; found himself saying "Thank you Carl."

Claire was next up, she and Tim gave a comprehensive overview of all their cases, including the case of the 'shovel wielding wife' as it was now being referred to by the team.

"It doesn't seem likely that this one will proceed to prosecution now Sir." she explained "The husband and wife both now agree that this was all an unfortunate accident." the sniggers in the room were audible, she

Justice

continued with a broad smile on her face "Yeah, it seems they were doing a spot of gardening at approximately eleven thirty on a Saturday night, as you do, in the dark and rain and that when she hit him it was 'completely unintentional'" she moved her fingers to indicate the wife's explanation for her husband's injuries. "Both had consumed quite a bit of falling down water when they were originally spoken to, as you know Boss," Both Tommy and Ishan were nodding their agreement, whilst the sniggering around the office continued to grow "and the husband does not wish to actively participate in any legal action being taken against his wife." She concluded.

"Previous?" Tommy asked, to which Tim confirmed there was no record of any previous domestic violence, at which point Tommy replied "Okay, so no complainant, no previous, lots of alcohol and I assume no witnesses wishing to do their civic duty and get involved?"

"No Sir." Tim confirmed.

"Then complete the paper work and let's get shut. We've got enough to do without getting involved in unnecessarily rocking the boat for loves young dream." he concluded with a smile.

Ishan quickly stood briefly and informed the team that as of now there was little to report on the apparent suicides of either Mark Bradshaw 39 or Annabel McKenzie 14 as they were awaiting the results of post mortems and the MAPP meeting was only taking place tomorrow.

Tommy openly cursed before he quickly looked around the room, his gaze landing on Tim. "Tim can you please chase up the Multi Agency Public Protection meeting please, it should have been done by now."

Tommy finally completed the briefing by addressing the team in his usual manner of clapping his hands together and issuing his familiar instruction "Right guys let's get to it!" before leaning in and quietly asking Ishan for a word in his office.

Justice

Once the door closed and they were alone in the office Ishan was surprised by how quickly Tommy's demeanour seemed to completely change, he was suddenly red faced and almost incandescent with rage.

"What the bloody hell is Foggy playing at?" he asked Ishan, but before he could even begin to contemplate formulating an answer he started barking a series of instructions. "You get down to that mortuary sharpish and tell him I'm bloody livid. Who in their right mind would prioritise the routine post mortems of three elderly deaths above those of a young man and a child?" he didn't really pause for breath as he continued "And you can tell Foggy from me I'm on the bloody war path, these families need closure, haven't they suffered enough? You tell him if his reports are not on my desk by this afternoon I will personal pay him a visit, and I can assure you Ish he does not want that!"

Sergeant Patel considered defending Dr Fogerty, who, it was widely accepted, was an excellent pathologist, a great colleague and a dependable friend. In his opinion

Foggy had performed a very difficult job with an unprecedented level of sensitivity and compassion for all those unfortunate enough to need his expertise for as long as anyone cared to remember. Ishan also wondered, for the first time, if Tommy hadn't returned to work too soon following his wife's death, after all it had only been a matter of weeks. He stood stunned into silence for a moment, contemplating what he should say and in the end decided to leave having said nothing.

A while later Ishan was still mulling over the extremely one sided conversation he had had with his boss whilst he was driving around the hospital site trying to find a parking spot within a decent walking distance of the pathology department entrance. He really hated having to drive through Manchester at the best of time, but the hospital was by far and away his least favourite destination. There never seemed to be anywhere to park and for some reason it always seemed to be raining as he arrived.

Justice

He had never seen Tommy so angry and although he understood the effect that dealing with the death of a child in any circumstances had on the team, he also knew that Tommy was the calming, supportive influence they all looked to whenever things got tough. He contemplated if he should speak to him about what had happened in the office. He was worried that his friend needed help and for the briefest moment he even considered speaking to someone higher up the greasy pole. He murmured a curse word to himself as he witnessed a space become available just three cars ahead of him only to be filled by a smug looking BMW driver, who seemed to deliberately make eye contact with him and smirk as Ishan drove level with him.

He had no idea what he could or should do to help Tommy but he did know that to avoid any further issues he needed to get the post mortem results as quickly as possible and as such, after 15 minutes of aimlessly driving around he decided, against his better judgement, to leave the hospital grounds and attempt to find that rarest of things, a side street not yet designated for the sole use of residents parking and run back to the hospital. The sky was getting darker and the rain heavier as he finally exited the car with a heavy heart, this was shaping up to be a right shitty day he thought, especially as he would be required to explain why yet another pair of expensive wool mix trousers required dry cleaning once he got home.

******

Tommy was sat in his office, which was little more than a small glass box, created by two prefab walls having been erected into the corner of a large, badly designed workspace; a series of old, dusty and faded, grey plastic, horizontal blinds hung at the windows, which, with their numerous broken or missing slats and their unfathomable cords, provided virtually no privacy. In reality it had never really occurred to him to complain or get the damned things repaired, he had always felt more at home in the much larger, open planned area, being visible to his team. He was catching up on some

Justice

of the more mundane paperwork that had been steadily building up for a while, or he would have been, if he wasn't just watching the rain hit the window like a mini monsoon, whilst contemplating how hard he had been on Ishan.

Ishan was such a warm, kind man and although he kept his work and home life separate, it was obvious from the few things that he said about his partner 'Em' that they were very happy together. Having someone to go home to, someone to talk to, to understand you and to love you warts and all, was he believed, the key to success in this job. He missed Cathy so much. A wave of physical pain seemed to suddenly overwhelm him like a tsunami, he was lonely and angry without her, he wondered about the man he was becoming without her endless patience and compassion, her guiding hand and wise counsel. As he continued to watch the rain through moist eyes he resigned himself to apologize for his bad behaviour towards Ish as soon as he could. He also decided to abandon all pretence of working; he would check on the team and take an early lunch. Once back he would have the PM reports and he and Ishan would have the unenviable task of meeting with the families of Mark Bradshaw and Annabel McKenzie again.

As if by magic at the strike of noon he found himself in The Three Bells, a traditional pub, if such a thing really existed these days, favoured by and predominately frequented by the local constabulary. Which was of little surprise, given it was owned and managed by a retired detective inspector and his wife and was situated less than a brisk two minute walk from the station.

"Hello Tommy love, how are you?" was the warm greeting that met him as he walked to the bar. He smiled at the older woman behind the bar, she was every bit the soap opera stereotypical landlady, small in stature and larger than life in personality.

Justice

"I'm doing alright thanks Ada, how's yourself?" before she had chance to answer a large booming voice filled the space.

"Sweet mother of god Tommy, don't be getting her started. She lives for someone giving her an opening like that." Ada giggled and gently hit the vast man, who had appeared, with the edge of a bar cloth she had been mindlessly caressing.

"Bill, good to see you." Tommy said.

"And you old man, now get yourself sat down and sorted, what'll it be?"

A little while later, filled with one of Bill's legendary, homemade shepherds pies, washed down with a cold glass of lemonade in front of a large open fire he was feeling so much more positive about life, 'it's the small things that make a difference' he thought to himself as he sauntered along the wet pavement. He felt contented for the first time in a long while, when suddenly this little bit of sedate normality was obliterated by the shrill ring of his work mobile. He retrieved the phone from his inside jacket pocket and looked at the unidentified number before answering "Detective Inspector Thomas Marsden."

Chapter 6

As he walked along the sparse basement corridor towards the pathology department, that seemed a million miles away from the hustle and bustle of the hospital above, Tommy could not shake the feelings of frustration. The call had been brief and yet clear, the pathologist had asked Ishan only to convey a simple request; that he attend the department in order to discuss an issue of some importance. It all seemed a little cryptic for his liking. From a very early age he had always been straight talking and unambiguous and to this day that's how he preferred others.

He wondered as he progressed along the warren like, meagre underground passages, which had once, long since, been painted a cream colour, if Ishan had actually been so stupid as to repeat their earlier conversation to Foggy verbatim and if he had, was the aged pathologist dragging him down here in order to reap some form of spiteful payback. As he moved quickly through dead spaces, one large plastic dividing door to another, his footsteps echoed on the concrete painted floor and the exposed pipes overhead reminded him of a horror film he had once seen starring Jack Nicholas, which had successfully troubled his sleep on and off for a couple of weeks as a teenager. As he neared his destination he realised the amount of junk, in the form of broken and discarded surgical appliances and old defunct looking machines was increasing. His mind was rushing ahead of him as he contemplated a number of scenarios in quick succession until he suddenly checked himself and decided to play this out as it came. There was absolutely no point trying to work out why he had been asked to attend and although it was a possibility that it was solely so the old man could seek vengeance for some off the cuff slight, in fairness that seemed out of character for the pathologist who always prided himself on his professionalism. No he decided; he wasn't here for his comeuppance following a minor insult in the heat of the moment. Foggy had never appeared to be in the

Justice

slightest what Tommy would call a small and petty man and he doubted if Ish would have delivered his message as harshly as he had received it anyway; his colleague was always so considerate with his words and on reflection Tommy was sure he would have been his usual polite and professional self with the good doctor. Nevertheless, this was proving itself to be at the very least an unusual situation and despite the annoyance and inconvenience at having been dragged across the city at this time of day, to defer to a phrase frequently used by his grandfather, 'his curiosity was piqued'.

Ishan and Foggy were huddled together behind a Perspex viewing window that separated a small office from the white washed, stainless steel world of the mortuary. Tommy entered from the left, off the main corridor; the familiar pungent smells he had come to associate with death instantly hit the back of his throat, causing him to give a slight cough as he acclimatized himself. He was static for a moment, before both men signalled in unison for him to continue walking along the right hand side of the room, which led to three steps that elevated the office slightly, allowing clear oversight of the entire clinical space.

As he entered he was greeted by the pathologist, Tommy quickly realising that if Ishan had conveyed his previous annoyance at the delay in receiving the post mortem results it had clearly had no effect whatsoever on the older gentleman as he set about his business.

"Ah, Tommy my boy, good to see you." He stood and smiled whilst simultaneously moving some papers from a tatty old chair and indicating he should sit down.

"What's the deal?" Tommy asked as he sat and adjusted his suit jacket, casting a disapproving eye over the stains on the arm of the once plush antiquated arm chair.

"Some good news and some not so good news for you, which would you like first?" the older man asked in his familiar congenial manner.

Tommy quickly glanced at Ishan who was sitting quietly in the corner of the cramped, shabby office "You know

Justice

me doc, hit me with some positives and we can take it from there." he replied.

"Okay...well the good news is that Sharon and I were able to work late last night and completed the PM's on both your apparent suicides." Whilst he talked he was rummaging around the office picking up various piles of paper and manila folders. Of course all the processes within the department had long since been computerised. All pertinent information being recorded in real time, via a quite advanced, some might say state of the art voice recognition computer programme, but the aged pathologist had a number of idiosyncrasies, the backing up of everything on paper being just one of them. Again Tommy looked towards Ishan who remained seated and decidedly non-committal, he shrugged almost imperceptibly as their eyes met, conveying he too was oblivious as to why he had been summoned.

"Ah. Mmm. Here we are!" he addressed the room as he pulled a beige folder from a pile resting on top of a dented old metal four drawer filing cabinet, that could well have been older than them all. In the following ten minutes the doctor went to great lengths to explain that there were no unexpected deviations in the examination or surprises in the findings surrounding the examination of Mark Bradshaw, and as such he eventually concluded that "given my findings, in conjunction with those of Sergeant Patel, namely a history of depression, the welfare concerns previously expressed by family and friends of non-compliance with treatments and supportive measures in place and the presence of a note, clearly outlining his intentions. I am satisfied that Mr Bradshaw's death was at his own hand and therefore I am happy to release his body to his family."

Tommy was silent for a moment, time appeared to stand still as the air within the room seemed to physically thin. He was confused to say the least. He looked in earnest at the doctor and then at Ishan before setting his gaze squarely on the older man's rheumy eyes.

Justice

"What?" he asked "What the hell is this?" he stood incredulous looking into the pathologists tired and washed out face. "Why the hell did you drag us all the way down here for nothing?" He became aware his voice was raised in line with his anger and he turned away, walking the few steps towards the back wall of the office to regain his composure.

Ishan became aware that the mortuary assistant, Sharon, had entered the examination area and was placing innocuous metal instruments onto dark green cotton cloths in preparation for the next examination. The room was eerily quiet for a moment until Foggy explained that the reason he had asked them to attend was not to receive the findings of Mr Bradshaw's PM but those of Annabel McKenzie which in his own words "Had proven to be rather less straight forward than could have been originally anticipated".

******

The tension in the room had already been palpable when Ishan cynically asked "So the 'good news' is a thirty nine year old man killed himself, leaving a pregnant wife and two small children?" he emphasised the word good.

"No! - The 'good news' is that this man can be returned to his family now and they can start to rebuild their lives following this horrendous tragedy" the pathologist replied quickly in his own defence, also emphasising the words good news within his sentence.

All three were suddenly silent, spent; the walls of the small room seemed to be closing in on Tommy as he closed his eyes for a moment to regain focus before looking at each of his colleagues. "Okay...Okay let's just calm it shall we?" quieter now he simply said "This isn't helping anyone." He took a deep cleansing breath before continuing "James," he said softly to the doctor "thank you for getting this sorted for us so quickly; and please pass on our thanks to Sharon for working late last night, I appreciate it."

Justice

They all knew the statistics on suicide; all wished it could be different but alas the number of deaths each year continued to rise. It was now widely accepted that suicide was the highest cause of death in men under the age of fifty in the UK. They also all knew that they were impotent in real terms and the only thing they could realistically do, was to return the deceased to those who would feel their loss greatest and longest as soon as was possible.

All three men returned to their seats where they sat for a moment in almost reverent contemplation, the only sound being the tools being placed in readiness by the mortuary assistant and the continual ticking of the wall clock, when suddenly as if a mask of professionalism descended upon them, bringing them back to the here and now, they continued with the task in hand.

Foggy stood and retrieved a further folder and commenced the reporting process by announcing Annabel's full name, age and date of birth whilst Tommy and Ishan listened intently.

When he concluded Tommy simply asked "Are you sure?"

"Yes, that's why I couldn't get the report to you any sooner. I ran the tests twice. Last night and again this morning" he explained.

"But she…"

"Please don't" the pathologist raised his hand and stopped Tommy before he could continue. He looked him in the eye and held his gaze "Please don't say she was 'only fourteen' or 'that she was from a good family, middle class, professionals, religious' or anything else Tommy. Please just don't".

It had been a very difficult afternoon and after thanking Foggy for his help Tommy and Ishan eventually walked solemnly through the desolate corridors towards the gloomy car park, each lost in their own deep thoughts. The cold evening air seemed to sting their faces as they emerged from the building. The rain had stopped but somehow it didn't seem to matter as they considered

Justice

the possibilities. Officially their shift had already ended, but in realistic terms neither believed they would be headed home anytime soon, feeling a burning need to return to the office, complete the necessary paperwork and above all try to understand what they had learned from the pathologist and how it may or may not have any bearing on the death of a young girl. They had already agreed that given the time they would visit Mrs Bradshaw and the McKenzies the following day when they were refreshed. As they slowly approached Ishan's car Tommy had an overwhelming desire to say something, anything, to his old friend about their encounter in his office earlier in the day. He respected Ishan, valued him as a friend and a colleague and it pained him to know he had behaved so badly towards him.

"It's been a trying day all round." he ventured with what he hoped was a remorseful smile.

"A bit of an understatement that, boss." was the humourless reply; but Ishan smiled as Tommy faded into the background in search of his own vehicle. That was probably the nearest thing to an apology he was ever going to get from his troubled friend, but that was fine by him.

Chapter 7

Much later, when Tommy finally arrived home and parked on the drive he sat in the car motionless for a moment and studied the building before him, it was in darkness and of course he knew it was empty, deserted. He suddenly dropped his head against the steering wheel, he felt exhausted. He missed Cathy so much that there was an actual physical pain within his chest, he felt hollow, a shell of a man. Of course work gave his life purpose, it always had, he understood that and currently it was his salvation. But ultimately at the end of every day, when he was alone there was a relentless massive void of nothingness for him to contend with.

As he entered the cold, shadowy house that had once been a vibrant, welcoming home he felt a shiver chill his very being. He fleetingly considered food, before almost immediately dismissing the idea and heading upstairs to once again experience the brutality of another night alone.

******

After a restless night he entered the station around seven thirty aware that he looked as tired as he felt. He had found himself tossing and turning throughout the night, unable to rest his body or his mind and in the morning the bathroom mirror had been merciless as he took stock of how he must appear to others. Admittedly a hot shower, shave and a decent suit had resulted in a measurable improvement but there was no denying the toll that Cathy's illness and loss had taken on him.

As he entered the office he was surprised to see that Ishan had already arrived and the two of them shared a lacklustre greeting ahead of the day. By nine o'clock the team was assembled and the daily updates had commenced. Tommy drank from a dark blue mug with the words keep calm and carry on emblazoned across the front as he listened to his colleagues. There were

Justice

few unexpected revelations so far and Carl was currently reminding the group he was expected to be available for court most of the following week as a result of an on-going case whereby a home invasion had gone south, resulting in life changing injuries to the unfortunate homeowner. Tommy took a sip of tea and pondered for a moment on the language used by the younger officer, it seemed like only yesterday the team would have been more familiar with a far more basic vernacular being used to describe how an unsuspecting pensioner had been burgled by the local pond life, who had successfully stoved his head in, leaving him paralysed on the left side and terrified in his own home. He often questioned the way in which politically accepted language seemed to diminish the crime and the victim, surely this was slowly eroding the effectiveness of policing. He felt tired and not for the first time he questioned the job. He recognised he was regularly out of step with 'modern policing methods' as his boss never shied away from informing him and over the last few months he had been feeling more and more like a round peg in a square hole, nothing seemed to fit. He questioned was he feeling this way because he was still grieving for Cathy? Would there come a time when he would no longer be grieving he wondered, or was he simply 'past it', out of touch and no longer effective? He was feeling old all of a sudden and he felt he was fast approaching some sort of crossroads in his life, the main issue with that was he had absolutely no idea what path to take and what his future would look like.

******

Once fully briefed on the current workloads Tommy put down his cup and stood as he addressed the group. "Okay...Ishan and I are meeting today with the widow of Mark Bradshaw. It seems pretty straight forward that this thirty nine year old male sadly died at his own hand and we expect the case to be closed following the routine administration." He paused for a moment coughing to clear his throat before continuing. "With regards to Annabel McKenzie, the fourteen year old girl,

Justice

we are meeting with her family at two o'clock to discuss the findings and possible implications of Doctor Fogerty's examination." He took a second to look around the room before he continued, his colleagues with the exception of Tim Jackson, who appeared to be furiously writing whilst holding a phone to his ear were looking toward him and listening attentively. "Due to his initial findings Foggy felt the need to perform a dual NAAT on our girl and it came back positive." The room was quiet and Tommy noticed that Tim was now off the phone and had joined the others in fixing his gaze directly upon him. Since the opening of a long awaited and greatly needed, 'stand-alone' unit dedicated to the investigation of sex related crimes and the support of victims across the North West, the team had had little involvement in the practical day to day management and investigation of criminal sexual violence, but they were all clued up enough to know that NAAT's or nucleic acid amplification tests were the fastest and most reliable method used to detect chlamydia trachomatis and Neisseria gonorrhoea. "So with both chlamydia and gonorrhoea present it appears we can be confident in assuming that Annabel was sexually active." he added unnecessarily.

"So where does that leave us?" Claire was the first to speak, but before anyone could answer Tim stated "Surely that's not too unusual today?" adding without missing a beat "Kids these days are maturing at a much earlier age than ever before, they are more aware of sex and lots are experimenting younger, I did a school attachment recently and quite honestly it was a real eye opener I can tell you-"

"Well that's as may be," Tommy quickly shut him down whilst recalling the words of the pathologist the previous evening, who had been keen to convey a non-judgemental attitude to Tommy when he had explained the results "but Ishan and I discussed this at length yesterday and given her age we are, of course, duty bound to investigate further. Obviously this is going to

Justice

be an extremely delicate matter when we meet with the family later today."

He looked around the room as he resumed "There are a number of things we need to consider here; firstly did Annabel have a boyfriend and if so who was it? Where her parents aware of any possible sexual relationships? Was any relationship she was involved in consensual? Or is there a possibility that she was the victim of some form of abuse or coercive control, possibly by an older person or persons as yet unknown. And finally what role does this new information play, if any, in her death?"

Tommy took a breath before recommencing "At this stage we have no evidence that Annabel did not knowingly, consciously and independently decide to end her own life, as was the natural working assumption given the circumstances. However, given this new information we also can't be sure that someone else didn't encourage, prompt or even assist in her death, so we need answers and we need them quick guys. Once we have spoken with the family again we will have a greater understanding of where this one is taking us."

Tommy became aware that Carl was now muttering something under his breath to Claire, who seemed to be trying to physically distance herself from him by slightly turning away, and he asked if he would like to share his thoughts with the entire team to which he replied "I'm just saying, in this kind of thing, well, it's usually the father isn't it?" Tommy knew that statistically Carl had a point and they would need to rule out anyone with a close relationship and unfettered access to Annabel, including her father, but he also refused to speculate further at this point and simply thanked Carl for his input before formally ending the team briefing.

Chapter 8

Sandy was busying herself in the kitchen, she was a naturally busy person and found it hard to sit and relax at the best of times, but in the last few days she had felt the need to be doing something all the time more than ever. As she emptied the dishwasher she shouted upstairs to her daughter for the third time that day to bring the cups and plates down from her room. She knew she was losing her patience far too easily with her daughter, but she just couldn't seem to help it. They had never let the girls eat in their rooms. They had always insisted that they eat at the table as a family, even when she was working late and John ordered pizza in it was still understood that they would eat in the dining room together, discussing their day and sharing quality time. "Quality time" she scoffed under her breath. They had been the very definition of good, caring parents with structured quality time built into their very existence, along with being approachable and in touch whilst remaining the reliable grown-ups their children needed. They had instilled a good work ethic in the kids from an early age and inspired and encouraged them to achieve and be their very best. Their girls wanted for nothing and as a family unit they were often envied by her friends, whose children were not as well-mannered or were less talented or not so naturally academically gifted. What good had it done them? What was the point of it all? Her baby was dead and try as she may she just could not understand why. She stood for a moment and her eyes automatically found that damned oak tree once more, as they so often had in the last few days.

When after five minutes Kirsty still hadn't answered or responded in any way to her repeated requests she was livid. Without thinking she almost ran to the bottom of the stairs and then proceeded to climb them two at a time exploding into her daughter's bedroom unannounced and seemingly unwelcome.

Justice

"What the hell?" Her daughter screamed as she burst into the room. She pulled her headphones off and stared open mouthed at her red faced mother.

"I have been calling you; I need you to clear all this mess up before the police arrive and there will be no more food and drinks in this room, you need to come down stairs and eat at the table like normal" she demanded, her voice was faltering her body visibly shaking.

"First of all, I couldn't hear you." Kirsty said as she held the headphones out from around her neck to emphasise her point. "And secondly, normal?" she sneered "Are you frigging kidding me!" she stood to meet her mother's gaze, her face contorted, eyes ablaze with the pure ferocity of her fury. "This isn't normal" she gestured around the room with both arms outstretched, "none of this is normal, for fucks sake mother!" she was stunned by the speed and ferociousness of her mother's hand against her suddenly throbbing cheek. She instinctively took a step back and studied Sandy before continuing "What difference does it make anyway if I have a few cups and plates in my room when the police visit? It's not like they'll be coming in here to see them is it? And even if they did, it's not bloody illegal is it?" She was screaming and shaking now, her voice scathing, every word wrapped in sheer vitriol as she continued "Jesus Christ is that really all you care about mother, keeping the house clean and tidy for all the visitors? Let's be honest shall we? Most of the people we have seen this week are just nosey, sad, pathetic, little creeps that want to feed off our grief and wallow in our fucking misery. But god forbid the house is not perfect, that we aren't perfect for the visitors! We wouldn't want to give the neighbours anything to tittle tattle about, would we Mother!" She suddenly collapsed on to the bed, her head falling forward into her hands, her natural curly, ebony hair providing a curtain to hide behind as she sobbed uncontrollably.

Sandy had instantly regretted slapping her daughter, she had never heard her girls swear and neither of them

Justice

had ever shouted at their parents. But that didn't justify violence and she was immediately besieged with an overwhelming sense of shame. She felt her entire existence was unravelling and that she was powerless to do anything about it. She was exhausted as she sat down on the bed next to her daughter and cradled her in her arms helplessly listening to her repeating over and over between sobs that nothing would ever be normal again. She rubbed her back in a circular motion, as she had when she was a small child, feeling inadequate in the avalanche of tears and snot as she simply repeated "I know sweetheart, I know."

******

Ishan had parked up in the tree lined street outside the 1930's mock Tudor detached house, which was set back from the road in a substantial, well maintained garden. "This is definitely what the estate agent would call desirable eh Tommy?" he said as he whistled through his teeth.

S. J. McDonald

"Absolutely, you'd need to do a considerable amount of overtime if you wanted one of these matey." Tommy replied as they walked up the driveway. They were just about to ring the doorbell when they suddenly heard raised voices and looking at one another, both instinctively stopped and listened. They couldn't hear the details of what was being said but it sounded like two angry female voices in a back and forth. After a couple of minutes the voices were quieted so Ishan rang the doorbell.

Mr McKenzie appeared after a short time "Good afternoon Mr McKenzie, Detective Inspector Thomas Marsden and Detective Sergeant Ishan Patel, I believe you are expecting us." Tommy said to the red eyed man still holding the door.

"Yes, of course, please, please do come in, please call me John." Mr McKenzie was approximately five feet six inches tall and slightly built; he had thinning ginger hair and wore thick black rimmed glasses. He seemed to be nervous and unsure of himself as he guided the officers

Justice

down a narrow, but pleasant, hallway into an immaculately decorated and well maintained sitting room. "Please take a seat and I will inform my wife you have arrived, would you like a drink?" Both replied in the affirmative and once their preferences had been established Mr McKenzie left the room ensuring he closed the door on his exit.

Ishan had met with the husband and wife when they had been required to formally identify their daughter at the mortuary, whilst Tommy had not had much contact since the initial conversations following the discovery of Annabel's body. But both had instantly come to the same conclusion; that Mrs McKenzie was the stronger of the two, likely to be more able to cope with any given situation and therefore more likely to be able to assist them with their enquiries.

As they sat in the deep, comfy arm chairs facing one another Ishan admired the cornflower blue Farrow and Ball paint which was perfectly complimented by the Lantern House, tree of life wallpaper and designer furniture, nothing had been left to chance in this impeccable space. They could hear muffled whispers, engaged in what seemed to be a furtive conversation and eventually the McKenzies joined them, sitting on a contrasting sofa between the two officers with a tray of tea placed on a low level occasional table directly in front of them.

"Good afternoon Mrs McKenzie" Tommy said as he made the formal introductions again.

"Please call me Sandy, everyone does." Her voice was confident and polite; however there was a definite hoarseness evident that betrayed her overall façade.

Once the tea was poured from a delicate bone china tea pot into equally fragile tea cups with matching saucers there was a brief hiatus before Tommy began to explain as sensitively as he could, that during the post mortem Annabel had been found to have had two sexually transmitted infections. Once the words were out they seemed to hang in the air, unregistered for a moment

Justice

until Mr McKenzie let out a slight whimper, reminiscent of a wounded animal, whilst he simultaneously seemed to physically crumbled before their eyes, folding in on himself where he sat, his wife went directly to his aid, standing above him, rubbing his back as he openly sobbed.

After a short while Sandy simply asked if they could be excused for moment and they both left the room, again closing the door.

The two sat in awkward silence once more until Ishan eventually said "See that wallpaper, over one hundred pounds a roll that costs. Em wants it for the lounge, but I can assure you we aren't getting it." Tommy smiled at the younger man. As far as he was concerned wallpaper was wallpaper and he had no idea how much it currently cost, but he remembered fondly how it had cost less than one hundred pounds to decorate the entire house when he and Cathy moved into their first tiny home together.

The sound of the door opening brought Tommy back to the present, Sandy McKenzie apologised for the delay and explained that her husband would not be joining them again as in her word he was "far too upset with this new revelation, on top of everything else to continue the meeting". She advised that she would inform him of any necessary developments later, when he would be more inclined to be able to process the information. With that the meeting was reconvened as she asked. "And you're absolutely sure about this Inspector?"

"Yes, I'm afraid so. I'm so sorry to add to your burden at this time, but given Annabel's age we feel obliged to discover how she acquired the infections. I'm terribly sorry but we will need to ask you some questions which may seem...insensitive, but unfortunately they are necessary if we are to fully understand what has happened to Annabel. We can take a break at any time you wish, just let us know." He attempted to reassure her with his words and demeanour, but realistically he

Justice

knew this would be the last thing anyone would want to have to hear following the death of a child. Sandy slowly nodded her head indicating both her understanding and willingness to proceed.

The meeting lasted for over an hour in total, with several short breaks during which Sandy basically closed her eyes for a second or two, gripping the sofa cushions, composing herself before answering anything asked of her. There was only one occasion where her emotions finally got the better of her, even then as she furtively wiped away her silent tears with a crumpled tissue retrieved from the sleeve of her well fitted navy blue dress, she asked if the officers would like more tea, collecting the tray, she had quickly exited the room under the pretence of normality.

As Tommy and Ishan finally walked down the drive towards the car, they were both impressed and concerned at her strength of character in equal measure.

"So what do you think about all that then?" Ishan asked as he was fastening his seat belt "It all seems a bit strange to me boss. His behaviour was very odd in my opinion; then there's the arguing we heard, that's got to have been the other daughter hasn't it?" he checked his mirrors and started the engine before continuing "We haven't seen sight nor sound of her as yet and don't get me started on the mother, I have never seen anything like it, she's a tough old cookie right enough."

They had not discussed it, there hadn't really been an opportunity to do so, but nevertheless both instinctively knew that the argument they had overheard within the family home may be an important development.

Tommy glanced at the house whilst listening to Ishan and sat quietly contemplating the visit before saying "I don't know Ish. Sure it wasn't what we would normally have expected, but in all honesty what is a normal reaction to the news that your child is dead and then us turning up to add insult to the proverbial injury?"

Justice

"Yeah, I suppose you're right" Ishan replied his furrowed brow and pursed straight lips obvious tells that he was in deep thought.

"Can you have a word with Lucy," Tommy asked referencing the head of the family liaison team. "I know they have offered some support but we probably need to see if they could do a bit more, given the current developments, it never hurts to have boots on the ground does it?"

Tommy used the continuing silence of the journey back to the office to consider the information they had obtained during their visit to the McKenzie home.

Chapter 9

Claire and Tim arrived back in the office around four thirty to find Tommy and Ishan waiting for them. Tommy was drinking from a white cup with a picture of a fish on the front and a message on the back that conveyed that Anglers do it online. It was one of a set of at least three he had encountered that included Rugby players do it with odd shaped balls and golfers do it in the rough. He had less than no idea where these cups came from, they seemed to just appear in the kitchen cupboard above the sink and he had never had the inclination to question their provenance or appropriateness for the office.

"Claire, Tim how did you get on?" Tommy had asked them to attend St Edmunds High School to work alongside and support the uniformed officers on site at the school where Annabel and her sister Kirsty were pupils.

Justice

"Not got a great lot to report to be honest Sir." Tommy watched as she consulted her note book, but her body language told him it was unnecessary. He also knew that if they had discovered anything of interest they would have told him before now.

"No boyfriend, she appears to have been a well behaved, smarter than average student. Parents are engaged with her education and always at school open events, parent's evenings, fund raising etcetera. There doesn't appear to be anything out of the ordinary in recent weeks. We spoke to a couple of girls that staff identified as friends, but they gave us nothing either." Tim stayed quiet and she seemed tired as she continued. "As expected we have mostly been engaged in the usual suicide contagion protocols, but we intend going back tomorrow when hopefully things may be a bit more organised. We have arranged to meet with some class mates from Annabel's form group tomorrow afternoon and spend some time with more of the staff and pupils on a one to one, so we may pick up some leads then. Uniformed colleagues have been allocated space in the sports hall and we've jumped in on that so we have a base to work from." she explained "The pupils and staff have mainly been addressed as a group so far and the whole thing has been mainly set to broadcast rather than receive. So sorry Boss, new information and leads are in extremely short supply."

Tommy had expected as much. Before they could get into the nitty-gritty of this specific case the insensitively named suicide contagion guidelines needed to be implemented. He still struggled with the concept of suicide clusters, but the evidence was unequivocal. Where someone in any given community commits suicide there is an overwhelming increase in the likelihood of others, in close proximity, either considering, attempting or actually committing suicide and of course he wholeheartedly supported any interventions that would prevent a cluster on his patch.

"Okay guys, thanks for that. Get yourselves off home now and recharge for tomorrow. We will meet as usual

Justice

tomorrow morning, but then I want you to concentrate your efforts down at the school. Do you currently have anything pressing that can't wait?" They confirmed they didn't and as they gathered their personal belongings together Tommy suggested that he and Ish also call it a day.

"Sounds like a good plan to me Boss." Ishan said as he was already clearing his desk.

Chapter 10

"Okay guys listen up." the office quietened almost immediately as Tommy stood to address the team. "We have a number of things that we need to consider going forward with the Annabel McKenzie case, but it's probably useful to recap on what we do know so far. Ishan, please?" He deferred to his colleague who stood in front of a green felt covered notice board which contained a number of items including a picture of a very young, almost angelic looking Annabel McKenzie. He pointed to the picture of the young girl as he started to speak.

"Right...So. We know that Annabel was a fourteen year old school girl that attended St Edmunds High School, along with her older sister Kirsty, who is in the sixth form college. Both parents are in the home, well-educated professionals and seem actively involved in the girl's lives, in a nut shell there doesn't seem to be anything too out of the ordinary within the home at this

Justice

stage." He took a breath; "The Multi Agency meeting hasn't flagged anything of interest. However, when we visited yesterday we did hear what appeared to be arguing, probably the mother and the older daughter. Is this new?" he paused for a breath before adding "Given the circumstances it would be totally understandable if it is, but we need to know if there are other, longer term issues going on within the family. Are arguments a regular feature in the home and if so, what are the reasons for them? Do arguments spill over into violence and what part has that, if any, played in this case?"

"As we all know Annabel was found hanging from a tree in the garden at the family home and no note has been found as yet. We also know that the post mortem examination confirmed sexual activity, namely basic physiology and the presence of STIs; what we don't know is who infected her. There are several things to consider here. Firstly, did she have a regular boyfriend, maybe of a similar age or older and if so who was it? Or are we potentially looking at a number of more casual sexual partners? What was the basis of any relationship? Remember guys that the law regarding the age of consent is in place to protect children and not to prosecute those couples under the age of sixteen who have mutually consented to sexual activity." He took another breath. "We will need to tread lightly at the school Claire if we want the kids down there to open up about anything they know or to tell us about any potential involvement."

"Understood." Claire lifted her head from her note taking to make eye contact as she spoke.

Tommy interjected "Claire, as well as digging around in the families background, you know the usual stuff, visits to A&E, suspicions that teachers could never prove and the like, I want you to speak with the sister too today please. Siblings often confide in one another and she may know something that could help us. Lucy Granger's team have been involved with the family, but given the shortage of suitably qualified family liaison officers it's

Justice

been a light touch thus far, so let's make sure we aren't missing anything."

"Yes Sir."

Ishan continued "So, in all honesty, we are not sure at this stage if this amounts to a criminal act that would lead to a prosecution. Obviously the issue of consent will need to be addressed regardless of the age of those involved."

He stopped to take a drink from the silver water bottle that always seemed to be on hand. "Secondly." he continued. "We need to consider the means of death in this case; hanging is not a commonly used method of suicide used by females of any age. Was Annabel assisted or encouraged to take her own life? If the sexual activity wasn't consensual it's not a massive stretch to see how someone else could have been involved somehow in her death." he hypothesised.

After a quick pause he added "If this death was in anyway assisted then that's a possible maximum prison sentence of fourteen years. If it's more than assisting...well who knows where this is leading us," Ishan sat back on the edge of his desk as he concluded. "And thirdly we need to be mindful of the fact that there was another suicide, by hanging on the same weekend as Annabel's death. We need to rule out any potential that this could be the start of, or part of an existing, suicide cluster. We need to take another look at the Mark Bradshaw case. Was there any point whereby the lives of these two crossed paths, and if so could this be an indication of a bigger issue for us?"

Tommy picked up the baton once more and asked Carl to do some digging into any possible connections between Mark Bradshaw and Annabel McKenzie. He continued as he made eye contact with each member of the team "Undoubtedly this is a complex case and as it stands we are still unclear as to whether a crime has been committed or not. But what we do know for sure is that we need answers as quickly as possible. Thanks everyone."

Justice

The background noise began to increase, as the team started to disperse. Tommy stood a moment and studied the photo of Annabel. She had a broad smile, flashing perfectly aligned white teeth; her straight dark brown hair was casually tucked behind her ears. He decided that she must have been looking directly into the camera lens when the image was captured, in that confident way that only the young and beautiful do. "What happened to you sweetheart?" he murmured under his breath.

Chapter 11

The school hall was cold and sparse, not too dissimilar to the one Claire remembered from her time at school. She was never what you would describe as one of the popular kids, she wasn't funny, cool or rebellious, she just kind of flew under the radar and got on with it. Although she had had some sympathy for the weaker, nerdy and the downright odd children she had rubbed shoulders with at high school she was far too busy to really care, dealing with her own anxieties and desire to 'fit in'.

She and Tim had arrived at the school by lunchtime following a visit to see Kirsty McKenzie, Annabel's older sister. As they walked along what appeared to be standard issue magnolia painted corridors, following the signs for the somewhat grandly named Student and Faculty Sports and Wellbeing Complex Claire was aware of her own footsteps echoing on the beige laminate flooring .

Justice

"My god don't you just hate these places?" she'd asked.

"What do you mean?" Tim smiled in reply and not for the first time she was a little too conscious of how handsome her younger colleague was.

"Well I can see how high school must have been tough for you." she teased "What, with your blonde hair and blue eyes. Bet you were sporty too. Most definitely in with the in crowd I reckon." she'd laughed.

"I did okay." He smiled again, showing even more of his perfectly white teeth.

She returned his smile as they continued silently down the corridor for a moment. Suddenly she'd wondered; was he flirting with her? And then almost immediately she questioned herself, was she flirting with him? She was his direct supervisor; she couldn't allow herself to be sucked into a situation she would undoubtedly regret. No surely it was nothing. Just banter between colleagues who were working closely together day in day out. Yes she decided that was all it was.

Nevertheless, as they had entered the sports hall she had been relieved to see the uniform officers busying themselves at their allocated desks within their makeshift 'command centre'. The tension she had inexplicably felt, had melted away as she made the necessary introductions and asked if the officers had identified any students they needed to speak with following their preliminary conversations.

It had been a very long two hours of dealing with crying children who, unsurprisingly all claimed to be have been the best of friends with the deceased. So far the information received was consistent in that: "Annabel was lovely person." "She lit up a room." "….Was beautiful inside and out…." And of course her kindness knew no bounds. But as yet there was no mention of a boyfriend, any kind of overtly sexualised nature or any comments or actions witnessed in recent weeks that would suggest anything out of the ordinary, nothing that would have indicated what was to come, there was nothing that might result in even the glimmer of a lead.

Justice

Claire was beginning to question the logic of the police contingent, who had attempted to mirror the open access approach of the counsellors also present at the school.

"Anything?" she asked Tim as they had a lull in demand.

"A big fat load of nothing I'm afraid." he replied "This is looking like a bust to me. What do you think?"

"Yeah, but it is what it is. Being out of uniform is not all high speed car chases and drug raids you know." She smiled at her partner who reciprocated, before rolling his eyes as he announced the arrival of some more young girls making their way across the sports hall with a simple "Oh God! Here we go again."

Claire and Tim took one girl each in to their respective makeshift cubicles, whilst two uniformed officers were engaging a small group that was suddenly forming.

Twenty minutes later, Claire was no further forward. Only having had it reaffirmed to her that Annabel was a wonderful, warm human being, by yet another young girl claiming to have been one of her closest friends. The look on Tim's face gave her the impression his encounter had been just as helpful as her own. She was just about to usher the next 'best friend' into the cubicle when one of the uniformed officers stepped into the space.

"You may wish to speak to this lad next Ma'am" she said indicating a boy towards the back of the group. Claire had been in plain clothes for more than two years, but still found it difficult when junior staff addressed her this way. She smiled reassuringly at the mousey young officer as she replied

"Yes, no problem and please call me Claire."

"Yes Ma'am. No problem, I mean Claire." She stammered, her slightly greasy looking skin flushing a little.

"And you are?"

Justice

"Siobhan, Siobhan Gallagher, Ma'am."

She saw that the younger constable was incredibly nervous and she didn't want to make things worse or stifle the lower ranked officers initiative by asking her a series of unnecessary questions about why she thought the boy should jump the queue, she was all too familiar with that type of behaviour from her own seniors. And in real terms it made no difference in which order they saw the children, they had to see everyone before they could even consider going back to the office.

As the PC had waved the boy forward Claire couldn't help but notice his confident swagger. He sat down opposite her with a bump as she proceeded, as required, to inform him of the process, namely that they had a number of set questions, but he could tell them anything he thought may be relevant. Before then seeking confirmation that he understood he wasn't compelled to speak to the police, whilst also conveying the seriousness of doing so and the importance of telling the truth.

"Can I ask your name?" Claire asked as she started to fill out a new form.

"Yeah, it's Pete Walker."

"You're a student here?"

"Yes."

"How old are you Pete?"

"Seventeen."

"That puts you in the sixth form, is that right?"

"Yes."

"And you were a friend of Annabel's?"

"Nope."

Claire looked up from the form and curiously studied the young man sat before her. He wore the obligatory grey hoodie, blue jeans and trainers, which, given the odd exception, seemed to be the unofficial uniform of the older sixth form students.

Justice

"So tell me Pete, how do you know Annabel?" she asked, watching closely as he replied.

"Well I don't, not really. I mean I've seen her around and I know who she is."

He was coming across as quite arrogant and for a moment Claire wondered if he was an attention seeker, someone who just wanted to have their five minutes of fleeting high school fame from the notoriety of being rebellious, of messing with the police. But she also noticed that one of his feet was tapping, heel to floor repeatedly at an increasing pace and despite trying to project a calm, even casual demeanour she believed he was either angry or anxious, she couldn't tell which, but she was sure he was emotionally invested and quite possibly had something of interest to share.

"So tell me Pete, if you don't really know Annabel why have you come to see me?"

"Because I know that creep she hangs around with, he lives just around the corner from me and I don't think it's right, it's not normal hanging around with a bloody school girl like that is it?"

Claire was aware of her own heart beat as she eagerly recorded the necessary details from Pete Walker, before discreetly interrupting Tim and asking if he had a minute.

"We've only gone and got a potential lead here." she whispered, unable to contain her excitement. "There's about another half dozen interviews to plough through as yet. What do you say we ask the PC's to complete the forms and get them to send them over to us, so that we can get back to base?"

"Sounds good to me." Tim replied "In fairness, if I never see another Kleenex paper handkerchief again in my life it will be too soon. I never expected the work to be 'all high speed car chases and busting drug lords.'" he said in respect of her earlier comments. "But bugger me! I really don't enjoy watching young girls crying for a living either."

Justice

"Great, you sort the forms and I'll finish up here." she said returning to her cubicle.

After Tim had spent ten minutes with the PC's explaining the finer points of the forms and the things they were specifically interested in, they were ready to leave.

"Good coppering Siobhan." Claire said as she turned to the now smiling uniformed officer.

As they exited the school Claire felt a warm internal glow, partly because they finally had a potential lead and partly as a result of the constables response to the praise she had received.

Once outside Claire quickly dialled Tommy's number as they were heading towards the car, it only rang once and before he could speak she announced "Boss, its Claire we're heading back, we have a lead."

Tommy and Ishan were waiting none too patiently in the office when they heard the external door bang open, quickly followed by the office door as Claire and Tim made their arrival known.

"What do we have?" Tommy asked before they could take their coats off.

"Nothing from the sister Sir, but a sixth form pupil has advised that Annabel hangs around with a bloke estimated to be late teens, early twenties. Bit of a loner apparently, described him as 'a bit odd' and a 'creep,'" The four looked from one to another in reaction to the description.

"And you have an address?" Ishan asked the anticipation building.

"I certainly do! Apparently, our helpful sixth former lives in the very next street." Claire continued. "He lives with his mother up in Didsbury, 22 St Johns Avenue. By my reckoning that's about four miles from the McKenzies. His name is Kelly. Not sure at this stage if that's his first or second name though."

"Okay...How do we want to play this?" Tommy asked.

Chapter 12

An Administrative Support Worker performed a quick review of the address against their system, which received daily and weekly updates from a number of places, including the electoral register, His Majesty's revenue and customs and The Home Office, but to name a few. The results indicated that two people lived at the identified address; they were a fifty-nine year old female named Lynne Jones and a twenty-five year old male named Oliver James Jones.

"No Kelly?" Claire asked with obvious surprise in her voice.

"Nope, not at that address." The rather rotund, Julie replied.

"Maybe the address isn't quite right. Maybe it's the wrong number?" Claire ventured hopefully.

"Well, I did a check of the entire street whilst I was on the system." Julie stated, whilst contemplating her long brightly painted nails. "No Kelly." and just for clarity she churlishly added "First or second name." She looked up from her desk at Claire and said "Would you like me to do the surrounding streets?" with what appeared to be a self-satisfied smile on her large round face.

"That won't be necessary at this stage, thank you Julie." Tommy interjected, he disliked how Julie often came across as a bit smug and had noticed, of late, that she appeared even more so whenever Claire was around. He made a mental note to speak with Julie about her attitude at a later date. But for now he had his hands full with a disappointed team and a visibly deflated sergeant.

******

"He seemed so convincing when he was telling me Sir." Claire said to Tommy, as she sat opposite him in his small and notably less tidy than usual office, later that

Justice

evening. "I bet that cocky little good for nothing toe rag is having a right good laugh at my expense right about now!" She seethed as she went to work on a hangnail on her right thumb, a habit which had resurfaced whenever she was stressed since early childhood.

"Okay...So tell me, why did you believe him?" Tommy enquired in his usual non-judgmental way.

She looked up into her boss's face, her eyes almost pleading for him to stop the analysis of her mistake.

"Come on, humour me, please." he held her gaze.

"Well," she began "the PC had singled him out for starters." she dropped her head forward again "Oh, I don't know boss, maybe I was influenced by the PC or maybe I just wanted to find us a lead so badly that I jumped on the first scrap offered up, like a hungry dog on a juicy bloody bone."

"Anything else?" He pressed on, his eyes had never moved and now he was looking directly at the crown of her head.

She could feel his eyes boring into her skull as she replied "Well, I suppose, if I'm being honest, what really convinced me was his body language boss, he genuinely seemed affected by what he was saying."

"In what way specifically?" he asked.

"Well, foot tapping really." she replied as she lifted her head, feeling foolish once again at how easily she had been taken in by the brash teenager.

Tommy swiftly stood and made his way around the messy desk to the office door in one seamless movement "Come on then." he said.

As they had made their way through the darkened, now vacant open plan office, Claire had no idea what was happening as she pulled her coat on and tried to keep up.

Justice

Now she was sat in an ultra-modern pub in Didsbury, aptly named The Enigma, which she assumed was in tribute to the late great mathematician and code breaker, Alan Turing. Despite the upper end furnishing and nicer than average décor she was feeling distinctly uncomfortable about their impromptu car journey, during which Tommy had not enlightened her on his thinking or the purpose of his spontaneity. She was trying to blend in with the other patrons, but she wasn't really sure what they were doing here. On arrival Tommy had gone to the bar and after some time returned with a pint of Boddingtons and a packet of nuts for himself and a diet Pepsi for her.

"You know you're a damn good copper Claire." He suddenly announced, as he settled himself into a brown faux leather tub chair and adjusted his jacket.

She had a feeling of impending doom 'Oh no. Please god no! He hasn't brought me here to give me a pep talk, to try and cheer me up, has he?' she thought as she gave him a meaningful look that she hoped he would take as a clear cease and desist request. She was mortified at the way things had played out, her foolishness. All she wanted was to go home and have a long hot bath, as she usually did whenever she felt anxious or overwhelmed.

But regardless of her obvious embarrassment, seemingly undeterred Tommy continued. "But, how many times have I told you, you need to follow your instincts?" he asked as she cringed inside. "I was just casually asking at the bar if anyone knows Kelly, who lives about half way up St Johns Avenue." Which he informed Claire was just around the corner before he added. "And the land lady said 'yes, but he's not in tonight.'" he smiled at her as he declared "Seems you were right Claire." He tipped his glass in her general direction, in a celebratory manner, before taking a long hard drink.

She was beaming as she quickly got to grips with this latest development and said "Okay so what's our plan Sir?"

Justice

They discussed tactics and had quickly finished their drinks before heading home. Claire was so excited when she finally fell into bed that she already knew she wouldn't be sleeping tonight. They had their first real lead in the case and she had been the one to get it!

Tommy was always telling her to go with her gut; that trusting your own judgement was what made for good coppering. She loved being part of the team and felt privileged to be working directly for Tommy, learning directly from him. He was a great role model and she desperately wanted to please him, to show him that his faith in her and her abilities had been justified.

She lay in the darkness, continually reflecting on the events of the day and listening to her own thoughts whirling, as a number of questions seemed to constantly churn around her head.

'Had Kelly been involved in a sexual relationship with Annabel? Was he the one who had infected her? If so was he also somehow involved in her death? Could he have actually killed Annabel? Why wasn't he found on the police system? What did he have to hide?' She sighed, releasing a long noisy breath and then smiled as she also wondered, 'exactly how good would it feel in the morning to stuff it to the ever pompous Julie?'

Chapter 13

Claire had been in the office for some time when Tommy finally arrived. "Coffee Sir?" she eagerly asked as he pushed the office door open. "Yes please." He had hardly replied before she'd scurried away into the small kitchen, returning with a purple cup with the word 'Boom' emblazoned across the front in the style of comic book.

They had agreed that they would attend the address of interest in search of Kelly during routinely accepted business hours, given that at this stage, they were only able to make basic enquiries and as he had reminded Claire several times last night, they had no reason to assume any wrong doing on the part of any of the occupants. Nevertheless, he sensed her enthusiasm and he too was quietly optimistic given the little they already knew about Kelly.

Following an unremarkable morning brief Claire and Tommy had once again headed out to Didsbury. They had hoped to miss the tail end of the rush hour traffic, but it was still slow going as they made their way across the city, sometimes at the pace of a steady crawl.

As they pulled up in front of number eighteen, two houses down from the address of interest, they took in the local surroundings. The neighbourhood was clean, tidy and well maintained. There were a couple of semi-detached, traditional looking family homes. But mostly the street contained impressive, larger than average detached houses in substantial, well designed, plentiful gardens. As they took in the view there was no denying that number twenty two was one of, if not the most imposing of the dwellings in this desirable location.

"Well, here goes nothing." Tommy said as he slid out of the passenger door to meet Claire on the pavement.

They approached the house with a mixture of emotions, they couldn't help but wonder if this could be the start of a break in the case that would help them better understand what had happened to Annabel and

Justice

eventually provide some much needed closure to her family.

There was a considerable delay from Tommy knocking and the door finally being answered by a somewhat dishevelled looking woman with dark, virtually black roots contrasting her almost yellow dyed, unruly hair. She was wearing what appeared to be an old silk kimono, which she pulled across her ample breast with one hand whilst simultaneously retrieving a cigarette from her mouth with the other. Her seriously chipped bright red nails were prominent against the almost unnaturally pale skin of her frail looking hands and for a moment Tommy was mesmerised by the image before him.

"Yes?" The voice was not as he had expected, it sounded refined, sophisticated. After just one word, despite appearances it was obvious that this person was educated, upper class or as Tommy's Grandmother would have said 'well to do'.

He was a little thrown as he made the necessary introductions, establishing that this was the home owner, namely one Mrs Lynne Jones.

"We are trying to locate a person called Kelly." He said, as he tucked his ID back into his inside Jacket pocket, returning his thoughts to the matter in hand.

"What on earth has that child done now?" She said without the slightest bit of interest or emotion denoted in her tone.

She considered the officers for a second more before opening the door slightly wider, allowing them entry and silently guiding them through an impressive entrance into a large sitting room, Tommy and Claire dutifully followed.

As they stood surrounded by some beautiful, yet clearly dusty and somewhat neglected furniture, paintings, and books, along with an assortment of grossly ostentatious objet d'art, Tommy wondered with a slight smile what Ishan would think of this interior décor.

Justice

Eventually the woman returned with a serious looking young man who extended his hand whilst stating "I believe you're looking for me." His voice was warm and inviting. Tommy wouldn't have called him handsome per se, but recognised there was something striking about his very presence. He was tall and slender with an undertone of muscle, yet when Tommy shook his hand he noticed his unblemished skin was soft and the interaction lacked the firmness he expected.

"Well that kind of depends. Kelly is it?" Tommy asked casually.

"No! No it is not!" The reply came from the woman now loitering at the edge of the room. She spoke slowly, over annunciating each word, as if to convey its importance, before adding "It's Oliver."

The young man looked uncomfortable as he flashed them both a forced smile and by way of an explanation he informed them that "Some people call me Kelly."

Once again Tommy introduced both Claire and himself, he studied the intriguing young man before him, as he asked if he had known a girl by the name of Annabel McKenzie.

"Of course I know little Annie." he had quickly answered.

"Don't say anything! Not another word. Do you hear me Oliver? I will get a hold of Theodor." the woman in the Kimono suddenly appeared awakened as she sprang into action; she continued "You know how you are Oliver, they won't understand. Don't say anything until you have spoken to Theodor." She pleaded.

"And how exactly do you know Annabel?" Tommy asked undeterred by the woman's protestations.

"He's not saying another word without our solicitor. Do you understand me?" she screeched in the general direction of the officers.

Justice

Tommy tried to ignore the hindrance of the piercing voice filing the room; focusing solely on the man they knew as Kelly. He knew they had one shot of getting his cooperation as he held his gaze, armed with the most endearing, harmless smile he could muster he had asked if Kelly would be willing to assist them in their enquiries, by answering some questions down at the police station. To which again the response was clearly given by Mrs Jones, this time in the form of a question "Are you arresting him?"

"No. Absolutely not. We would just like to speak with Oliver as a potential witness. If he knew Annabel he may be able to help us with some questions we have, he may have witnessed something or heard something that could help us-" Tommy was cut short.

"Can you please leave my house? He's not going anywhere!"

Tommy turned slightly towards Claire and although they would continue to try and persuade the man to assist them for a few more minutes, realistically they both knew this line of enquiry was all but terminated already.

Chapter 14

"Any thoughts?" Tommy asked of a silent and clearly contemplative Claire as their car slowly exited St Johns Avenue.

"I'm not sure Sir to be honest. Obviously he said he knew Annabel, but exactly how their lives would have crossed paths in any meaningful way is beyond me."

"I know what you mean, the age difference rules out them meeting at school, even taking into account if he had attended the sixth form..."

"He's obviously hiding something." Claire interrupted his train of thought, as she scratched away at the inside of her right thumb with her index finger whilst simultaneously holding the steering wheel, a clear indication she was feeling frustrated by their disappointing encounter.

"Well, his own mother certainly seems to think he's got something to hide, so that's interesting to say the least," his eyebrows raised as he spoke "but as it stands we have literally nothing to link him to anything, there's no evidence of any wrong doing." he took a long calming breath before continuing. "So as it stands we currently have no legitimate reason to take him into custody or even speak to him without his consent or should I say his mother's consent" Tommy reminded Claire sourly.

"Don't you think we should have lifted him, whilst we had the chance Sir?" She asked.

"No. He'll keep for now. We know where he is." Tommy said "There is very little point bringing him in if he's not cooperative. No; what we really need is to regroup and try and establish what the hell we are looking at here!"

They mulled over every detail of their visit on the way back to the station, but in fairness, as they climbed out of the car they were both painfully aware that they were no further forward now than they had been before the visit.

******

Justice

Ishan was sat at his desk typing as they entered the office. As he looked up from his keyboard he couldn't help but notice that both Tommy and Claire looked a little despondent. "So, did we find the mysterious 'Kelly'?" He asked.

"We most certainly did." Tommy replied "And if you would be so kind as to fix us both a nice cup of coffee, we will enlighten you thus far." The level of sarcasm was palpable and Ishan could almost hear Tommy's eyes rolling as he spoke.

Once Tommy had a cup of coffee in his hands and Claire had done the honours of reliving the details of their earlier encounter, the three of them set about reviewing what they did know in the hope of identifying their next actions. This was a well-practiced method used frequently by the team, which had proven invaluable on countless occasions.

"So there's no chance they met at school?" Ishan asked.

"No. Doesn't appear so," Claire answered, adding "we're not even sure if he attended St Edmunds."

"Claire, find out if he did and if so, see if there are any specific events whereby ex-pupils would be engaged with current pupils. Maybe there's some kind of buddying or mentorship programmes, or something." Tommy was thinking aloud in between sips of his now cooling coffee.

"Yes sir." Claire was studiously recording into a small black note book.

"And the location of his home in relation to the McKenzies house, could they have simply bumped into one another?" Ishan continued.

"It's not really that close in practical terms, they aren't exactly what you would call neighbours." Claire explained, before concluding "I think it's unlikely they would have met by accident on the street, but even if they had, Annabel was apparently a smart girl. Which

Justice

fourteen year old girl is going to just befriend a twenty five year old, male, total stranger on the street?"

Tommy nodded in agreement "I see your point Claire, but it's not impossible, as we all know only too well, people with nefarious intentions can be very resourceful." He didn't need to elaborate further. He placed a large rough hand over his mouth for a brief moment, rhythmically tapping his fingers against his cheek, before he spoke again "Ishan, the family didn't identify any possible places, whereby our girl may have met this Kelly fella, did they." It was a statement rather than a question. "To my recollections" he continued "they said she only really attended school. She had piano lessons, but that was with a female tutor within the home. There were no clubs or regular social events. So where the hell did they meet and what exactly was the nature of their relationship?" he pondered on the seemingly elusive questions once more.

Ishan confirmed Tommy was correct in his thinking, the family had been clear that Annabel wasn't a member of any groups, before adding only that "St Edmunds School, has a close relationship with the local church, could she have met this Kelly that way?"

"Good thinking Ish, could you call in on Father Mark and follow that up for us?" Tommy asked.

"Sure."

The group were quiet for a further moment when Claire suddenly asked "Did we get the report back from the techs regarding Annabel's phone and laptop yet? However she met him and regardless of their relationship they had to be in contact somehow. Didn't they?"

"One would assume so, but if it's a regular meet, same time, same place kind of thing then maybe not. I asked Carl to put a rush on the devices, but I haven't heard anything as yet and he's been in and out of court this week. Could you chase that up as well Claire please?" Tommy asked. He then turned to face Ishan directly,

Justice

before explaining "You and I will need to visit the family again."

Chapter 15

The coroner had formally opened and then immediately adjourned the inquest in to the death of Annabel McKenzie. This had been expected, as it was common practice in a case of this nature, where the police were still actively investigating the circumstances surrounding the cause of a death.

Families almost always viewed this situation as both good and bad news in equal measure. Good news in that the deceased could finally be laid to rest and they themselves could achieve some form of closure. Bad news in that a full inquest would be looming over their heads, for what could be a considerable amount of time to come, in effect negating any chances of them finding any real peace or closure for the foreseeable future.

As usual Sandy was trying to be positive, they could now arrange a service befitting her beautiful daughter, and at the exclusion of anything else, that was what she was currently busying herself with.

Justice

When she had been contacted by the police the previous afternoon they had agreed to a meeting at eleven o'clock, as she had a prior arrangement to meet with the Priest from St Edmunds at ten to finalise the details of Annabel's funeral.

******

Tommy and Ishan were walking through the small, immaculately maintained wrought iron garden gate towards the McKenzie home at precisely eleven, when the front door opened to reveal Mrs McKenzie and Father Mark, who appeared to be saying their goodbyes.

After a brief moment the white haired gentleman turned his attention towards them.

"Good morning Inspector, Sergeant." The exiting priest greeted them both.

"Good morning Father." They replied in unison, like naughty children caught in some deplorable act.

S. J. McDonald

Tommy felt awkward in the presence of the kindly old priest. Over the last few years he could have been described, at best, as a fair-weather parishioner, making only the odd appearance in church outside of weddings, baptisms, funerals and Christmas, but since Cathy's funeral he had been unable to muster even the slightest interest in the church; in fact he had openly shunned all the offers of support and assistance made by the considerate aged gentleman before him.

"How lovely to see you Tommy. I haven't seen much of you in recent times." the clergyman said in his usual jovial manner, as he peered over his metal framed spectacles. For as long as Tommy had known him he had always looked over his glasses whenever he seemed to be gently chastising someone, it was such a common occurrence that at times Tommy had wondered if he actually needed them for seeing or if they were merely a prop.

Justice

"No Father, I've been sort of busy. You know how it is." Tommy slipped a finger into his shirt collar to ease his apparent discomfort momentarily.

"Yes of course, of course you have." he took a slow deep breath "Still, it would be lovely to see you in church now and again my boy. When you have the time of course."

Tommy smiled down at the much smaller and recently frail looking old man, as he quickly performed a mental recalculation of his daily tasks before replying "Funny enough, Ishan and I were intending to call in on you later this afternoon if that's okay?"

The older man smiled warmly, readjusting his glasses as he said "Splendid. Splendid."

Both Tommy and Ishan knew that the visit to St Edmunds hardly warranted the presence of one senior officer, let alone two, however, both had also recognised some time ago that they were no match for the wily Father Mark.

S. J. McDonald

Once the arrangements for their visit to St Edmunds Church were made, they were warmly greeted by Sandy McKenzie, who, as always, was running a tight ship.

Chapter 16

They walked through the churchyard, taking in the imposing building with its magnificent masonry and large colourful stained glass windows at precisely noon.

"Good job Mrs McKenzie always has cake and biscuits on hand isn't it Sir, we've probably kissed goodbye to any chance of lunch now eh?" Ishan said with a warm smile whilst giving Tommy a knowing look.

"Sorry, what's that?"

"Just saying, no telling how long we will be here and what 'good deeds' Father Mark will try and strong arm us into whilst he's got us."

"Err. Yeah. Probably."

Ishan decided to quell the conversation, as they made their way towards the opulent, yet noticeably cold vestry to the left of the main body of the church. He could see his friend was distracted, understandably so, he thought.

"Tommy, Ishan how lovey to see you!" the elderly clergyman stood, greeting them as if it had been years since their last encounter and not, as in reality, slightly over an hour.

Neither expected much from their visit as they settled in next to a decrepit, electric heater, the two exposed orange bars of which, gave off a glorious orange glow and very little warmth.

"Bit nippy in here Father." Ishan said, rubbing his hands together, aware of his breath as he spoke.

"Yes, it is a bit of a nuisance I'm afraid. Of course I just put on an extra cardigan, but it's not good for some of the older members of the congregation as you can imagine." He looked from one to another, over his spectacles, before explaining that St Edmunds was feeling the pinch, like everyone else, with the high cost of energy and had had to adjust the heating accordingly.

Justice

"Of course we are engaging in a number of fund raising events to try and assist with the heating issues, but I shall not bore you with the details." He studied both officers again whilst adjusting his glasses.

"So," Father Mark asked, with his usual congenial smile "how can I help you two fine gentlemen today?"

"We have some questions about Annabel McKenzie." Tommy replied.

"Oh yes, of course, terrible, terrible business. Very sad."

"Did you know Annabel well?"

"A little, she was a nice girl from what I do know. These days the school children are here less and less, Christmas, Easter, Harvest Festival and the likes," he said in way of an explanation. "The McKenzies are good people, but they have busy lives. The mother is a nurse you see and work gets in the way, well, you know how it is." He looked pointedly at Tommy, who cringed inside momentarily.

"Do you know a young man by the name of Oliver Jones?" Tommy asked quickly to divert the man's attention.

"Oliver Jones...Oliver Jones..." he muttered to himself for a moment "Yes, I remember him. Not much to tell really. He attended Sunday school until about the age of ten and not much since."

"Could he have met Annabel here do you know, through some social or community event, if not the church itself?"

"That's highly unlikely; I oversee most of the activities personally you see. No. I'm sorry. Like I say Annabel was only involved with the church under the direct supervision of the school and Oliver doesn't attend any more." he paused for a beat. "What I do remember is that the mother was a bit of a strange character."

"In what way?" Tommy asked; keen to get another perspective on the woman.

Justice

"Well. Overbearing, quite demanding really. In the Oliver needed to be Joseph in the Nativity kind of way, that's not unusual of course" he gave a tight, forced smile "but I remember she was a little more dramatic than most when she wasn't getting her own way. I don't know, what is it they call it these days; entitled?" He looked at his visitors as he tried to explain. "She just seemed a little over the top at times." Tommy knew what he meant, whatever it was called these days; it was definitely an undesirable quality.

Ishan, who had been quiet in the main since their arrival, suddenly asked "Why is he also known as Kelly, do you know?"

"Honestly, I do not. But I remember there was quite a fuss, some while back about it. Stuff and nonsense I'm sure."

"What was the issue?" Ishan pressed the priest.

"Just silliness really. A rumour, nothing more, however, I can tell you a couple of the older parishioners were quite discombobulated for a number of weeks at the time. They got themselves into a bit of a state," he chuckled "I remember I had to deliver a sermon about baseless gossip in the end. You know how quickly these things can travel around the community. I often say if only the word of God travelled half as effectively as idle gossip, I'd be out of a job." He chuckled to himself again. "Anyways it seemed to calm down as quickly as it started, as these things so often do."

"What was the rumour?" Ishan pressed further.

"Well, apparently there was this serial killer called Kelly in America around the time Oliver first started calling himself Kelly, and somehow, who knows how these things come about, it was rumoured that he admired this killer and wanted to emulate them. Like I say ridiculous rumours. Absurdity. Nothing more."

Ishan was stunned, his blood chilled, he knew only too well the damage that unsubstantiated rumour could do

Justice

to a case. But on the other hand he wondered if there may be something to this crazy story.

An hour later, as they were leaving the church grounds, having been alleviated of twenty pounds towards the heating bill, they were acutely aware that not only did progress appear to be non-existent in this case, but that they were amassing more and more questions at every turn.

Chapter 17

"I have found only one reference to a serial killer called Kelly and that's a woman. But according to this article on the internet, Kelly Crane may have killed up to nine people in America, including her husband. It says here that she is believed to have killed at least one of her lovers and it was reported that she may have had some cannibalistic tendencies too, having allegedly put human flesh on a barbeque and served it to her neighbours at a get together of some kind." Ishan was reading from his phone as Tommy drove.

"Jesus, Ish, have you nothing better to do?" Tommy glanced at his colleague. "We could do with one less blind alley down which to travel, wouldn't you agree?" his frustration clear. "We're all over the bloody place with this one and when all's been said and done we're not even sure if a crime has been committed," he inhaled sharply and immediately puffed out a gasp of air "all we have at best is maybe one person of interest,

Justice

that we aren't even in a position to speak to under caution yet, so let's not start running away with fanciful stories or potential serial killer wannabes, shall we?"

Ishan looked at his boss "Hungry?" he asked.

"Starving."

"The Bells?" Ishan said, in reference to The Three Bells pub, which they frequented as much for the traditional homemade fare it served than anything else.

"That's the best idea I've heard so far today."

They knew that even though it was way past lunch time the gamely landlord would accommodate them, as he always did.

******

After placing an order for one scampi and chips with extra tartar sauce and one steak and ale pie and chips with extra gravy the couple took their usual seats, close to the open fire which was both warming and inviting.

S. J. McDonald

"I reckon old Father Mark could do with this in his vestry, eh Sir?" Ishan said as he held his palms out towards the blaze, revelling in the warmth as it flooded his body, his face illuminated in the dancing colourful flames. "That electric heater he uses is nothing short of a health and safety nightmare isn't it?" When he got no reply he looked from the fire to see a grinning Tommy struggling to contain his laughter.

"What?" he asked in all innocence.

"Dear God Ishan, you're not telling me you bought that poverty stricken old priest routine, with his two bar electric fire and his extra cardigans are you?" he said with a knowing look.

"You mean-" Ishan started but was quickly stopped by the simultaneous arrival of their food and a resounding "Yes!" from Tommy.

"Can you believe this Bill?" Tommy asked of the large, Irish landlord who was delivering their much needed food.

Justice

"What's that then?" Bill asked in his distinctive booming voice with its still prominent accent, whilst placing the plates down carefully onto the sturdy old pine table.

"Old Father Mark, at St Edmunds, had us over again today."

"Not the old 'I can't afford the heating' scam surely. He was pulling that when I was on the job." He laughed as Tommy nodded his confirmation "Oh, Ishan. I can't believe you fell for all that baloney. It's just Father Mark's way of getting some coffers out of the Sunday 'no shows' to help fund the new roof. Always best to just play along and cough the money up lad. You go when he's not expecting you and it's always nice and toasty!" he laughed "Mind you, if you do go when it's warm, then he gets you for the actual roof repairs!"

Both Tommy and Bill could no longer control themselves and burst in to fits of raucous laughter as a forlorn Ishan announced "But, he took me for a tenner and I'm not even a Christian."

Chapter 18

They had just about finished their very late lunch, come early dinner and were feeling so much better for having a full stomach when Tommy's phone had begun to ring.

"Here we go again." he smiled at Ishan as he fished it from his inside pocket "No rest for the wicked, as they say."

"Boss, it's me. Where are you? We've got him!" an overly excited Claire declared.

"What? Hang on a minute, what's happened?" then on second thoughts he said "Alright, calm down, we will be in the office in five minutes, you can tell us then."

As they arrived Claire was stood in the office like a caged animal ready to pounce, continually staring at the old wooden door in anticipation, almost willing it to open.

"What's going on?" Tommy asked.

Justice

"The techs have sent me their report on the findings from Annabel's phone and lap top. There's nothing of interest on the laptop but there's some crazy shit on the phone boss. Evidence of some sort of an on-going relationship at least between Annabel and Kelly, some of the messages are pretty dark too."

Tommy was taking off his coat as he heard Ishan ask "Is there anything sexual?"

"I haven't seen anything sexually explicit as such yet, but the messages between them are a bit strange. The ones I have seen are bizarre. It's hard to explain," she said "they're definitely weird and there's an odd kind of fixation on death too."

Tommy was fired up, if there was a sexual element to the relationship between Annabel and the guy they referred to as Kelly then given Annabel's age that was one crime they needed to pursue, if there was any reason to suggest assistance or coercion in her suicide that was another. He also considered for a moment what Father Mark had said earlier today and wondered if it was possible that Kelly could have acted out some kind of fantasy he may have had around murder. Clearly they needed to fully understand what the technical team had found. "Right, first things first," he said "whose turn is it to brew up? If either of you two lovely people have any plans for tonight, then I would strongly suggest you cancel them now. We need to see what we actually have here, but this could be an actual break at last."

******

The office was alive with expectation and promise, although it was pitch black outside now and they were finding it hard to decide who was responsible for making yet another cup of coffee and whether or not they should order take-out food, the one thing that had required no discussion and yet they were all agreed upon, was that they would keep working for as long as it took, until they understood what they were actually looking at.

Justice

"It's some kind of code isn't it, some kind of secret language between the two of them?" Claire said her head bowed, fingers interwoven with a mass of unruly dark brown curls that appeared almost black in the half-light casting its shadows.

"These messages have been going back and forth for more than two years, so obviously they have had a long term relationship of some sort, how on earth could her parents not have known about this?" Ishan asked no one in particular before continuing to speak "...but even now we have the messages it's hard to know what's what. Some of it appears completely innocuous, run of the mill stuff. 'How are you?' 'What are you doing?' 'Shall we meet at the edge?' and then there's everything else that makes no sense what so ever!"

Tommy looked up from his copy of the report, Claire had had the presence of mind to make three copies before they had arrived, knowing only too well that they could no more have performed this process on a computer screen, than they could have ridden a unicycle to the moon and back. "'The edge', have we any idea what that is yet?" he asked.

"Not really, no." Claire replied, reaching for a piece of paper. "I ran a search earlier and it's come back with three possible matches to the name in a ten mile radius of the McKenzie home. But, to be honest, none that a 14 year old girl would have regular access to, if you know what I mean."

Tommy glanced at the list which contained two gentleman's clubs, The Edge of Paradise and Closer to the Edge and a company called Living on the Edge that claimed to be specialised in the marketing of vouchers for life experiences and bucket list must do's. He raised an eyebrow as he said "We had better check them out any way, you never know."

"These text messages are strange, they don't appear to make any sense, I think your right Claire, I think it's a code of some sort." Tommy said, as he started to read them again for the umpteenth time, picking out some

Justice

of the more obscure ones in the hope of discovering the key and deciphering the meaning of them.

I have immortal longings in me.

The way to a dusty death. Out, out, brief candle!

Remember life is but a walking shadow.

For in that sleep of death what dreams may come.

To die, to sleep

I will kiss thy lips

There was easily five pages worth of the obscure messages and it seemed to Tommy that they are evenly split between both Kelly and Annabel being the sender and the receiver. He flicked through the pages once more, the words and letters becoming a little blurred, whilst they continued to mean less and less to his tired eyes

"Anything? I will literally take any suggestions right now. I'm completely stumped." He said as he leaned back in his office chair trying to stretch his aching back a little for what seemed like the thousandth time in the past few hours.

"No, sorry I have nothing." Claire answered.

"Yeah, same here I'm afraid, I've nothing either." Ishan said "I think we should bring him in."

"On what grounds exactly?" Tommy asked, playing devil's advocate.

"Well, it's clear he knew her." Ishan replied.

"Which he never actually denied" Tommy reminded him.

"Well on the grounds that he called her 'his little orphan Annie' and she calls him 'her sweet prince'. Given the circumstances." Ishan continued.

"Correct me if I'm wrong. But last time I checked, it's not illegal to have a pet name for a friend or associate." Tommy's voice was calm and calculated as he further

Justice

pushed the team to develop a compelling theory they could work from.

"She's talking about kissing him." Ishan was becoming desperate to make a point that they could possibly act upon.

"Again, granted, extremely unsavoury, but in and of its self not an actual offence." Tommy countered

"They're talking about death. On the second page he even talks of 'tying a noose like a necktie for a fancy ball' for god's sake!"

"You're right they are both talking about death." Tommy emphasised the word both.

"But she's the only one dead isn't she Tommy!" Ishan was at the end of his argument; he was desperate but had nothing else to give.

Tommy looked towards Claire who had been quiet throughout the exchange. "What do you think?" he asked.

"I think we have probably got what we're getting. We don't have any other leads at this point, do we? I'm sorry but I agree with Ish, we probably need to bring him in and sweat him a bit, hope he gives something up."

Tommy leaned back in his chair once more, contemplating the once white ceiling tiles for a moment, before saying "Right then, let's get home and get a couple of hours rest. We can bring him in tomorrow morning."

Chapter 19

The team were visibly anxious; the office notably quieter than usual. It was eleven o'clock already and they could still hear through the wall, the remnants of what had been, at times, a heated discussion between Tommy and his superior Richard Stephenson. The Detective Chief Inspector was known for being a rather surly and officious, bad tempered man; and the ever disagreeable Stephenson had been putting Tommy through the ringer throughout the morning, periodically asking that he be allowed to check something or other before ringing Tommy back.

As he emerged from his office Tommy couldn't help but notice the body language of his colleagues, he too felt the pressure of the morning so far.

"Where are we?" Ishan asked

"Honestly, I'm not sure, it could go either way. You know Dickie." He stood with his hands on his hips, trying, unsuccessfully to appear a little more confident than he felt as he continued. "He's concerned about the quality and amount of evidence we have. He's also concerned that the text messages we do have are addressed to a person named in Annabel's phone only as 'Kelly' and that there's no mention of an Oliver James Jones anywhere."

Ishan opened his mouth to speak but changed his mind as Tommy continued "And don't get me started on the proposed charge. He's having a god damn field day with that." Tommy looked skyward for a moment.

"Yeah, I get it. I really do, but we have to go with what we've got and assisting a suicide was our best chance of bringing him in, given the messages we've found on her phone." Ishan explained.

Tommy nodded "I know, but if we do, by some miracle, get the paperwork sorted out on this one, we will be relying on this Kelly fella giving us more than we currently have and that's never a good situation to be

Justice

in, as well you know." He took a deep breath as he continued to consider their current position, weighing up the possible outcomes. "Well," he finally said "we are where we are, as they say. We don't have any other leads, so we need to play this one out to the end."

They all knew that without the cooperation of their overtly cautious, extremely bureaucratic superior they literally could do nothing. Tommy hated that Stephenson demanded that almost every slightly contentious decision was run past him personally. His autonomy to act as he saw fit, to lead his team, was being drastically eroded on a daily basis by the chronically risk averse, loathsome little man.

The team watched as Tommy retreated back to his office and again picked up the phone.

Tommy knew they didn't have much to make a case and what they did have was an almighty stretch. But what he did know was that a grown man had been having clandestine meetings with a child later to be found to have had at least one sexual encounter, that same child had later been found dead, following a hanging, which may or may not have been connected, but the balance of probability was tipping towards this fella being guilty of some sort of wrong doing, of having committed at least one heinous deed and as such Tommy knew he couldn't risk just leaving him on the streets, unabated, the risk was too great. Tommy also knew that if things didn't go well, he and he alone would be held accountable. He was suddenly reminded of a phrase his grandmother had frequently used when he was a boy 'He who pays the piper calls the tune' she had frequently said and he smiled for a moment.

As he waited for his call to Stephenson to be answered, his only hope was that if this didn't pan out that the price he would be required to pay wasn't going to be too high.

Chapter 20

The team had been shocked at the dramatic turn of events when just before lunchtime a rather ashen looking Tommy had suddenly emerged from his office and announced, "Ishan, Claire, go bring him in." Before turning to the administrative support worker, saying "Can you make sure interview room four is available please Julie?"

"What do you think tipped it for us?" Claire asked as she and Ishan crossed the car park.

"Whoever knows?" he mumbled, whilst simultaneously trying to supress concerns about the negotiations and likely compromise that may have been necessary in exchange for the green light.

Less than an hour later, Oliver James Jones, known also to them as Kelly, was securely ensconced within the whitewashed walls of interview room four. Room four was favoured by most of the senior officers, as it was far and away the best equipped room and the observation area was without doubt the most comfortable and spacious; as such it was usually reserved for those suspected of the most serious of offences, for which the interview process was frequently a considerably prolonged affair.

"He's in four and good to go Sir." Ishan reported as he hovered at the door to Tommy's office.

"Has he asked for a solicitor or anything?"

"No, he's not asked for anything. To be honest, he's playing nice so far, very cooperative, very pleasant."

"Good. Right then, let's leave him for half an hour and then you and Claire can have a run at him. Let's see just how cooperative he is once we start asking some difficult questions."

"Okay will do" Ishan said as he closed the office door, leaving Tommy to his own thoughts.

******

Justice

Staring at her reflection in the mirror of the ladies toilets Claire was under no illusion this was the longest thirty minutes of the day. She glanced at her watch again, "bloody hell" she whispered to herself, she was beginning to question the possibility that time was actually running backwards as she sighed aloud. She felt completely overwhelmed, her mind in a state of flux. She had only tolerated a couple of yoga lessons, finding the stuck up, self-absorbed instructor too obnoxious to endure, but from what she remembered, the key to calm and inner peace was to breath slowly whilst keeping your feet flat on the floor, in….out….in….out…

After a couple of minutes, that seemed like a life time, she had to face facts as she scrutinised her appearance once more and told her reflection quite bluntly that this wasn't working. She could almost hear Tommy's voice against the backdrop of water cisterns filling - 'good coppering' he used to tell her is all about working well together, anticipating one another's next move, ensuring you were both on the same page. She slipped her shoes back on and straightened her jacket before exiting the loos and walking purposefully in the direction of Ishan's desk.

"You okay?" he asked as she sat in the chair at the side of his immaculately maintained desk.

"Yeah. You?" She tried to sound light hearted, casual. She never ceased to be amazed by how organised Ishan was, his workspace was never cluttered like hers so regularly was and also unlike her, he always looked like he'd just stepped off the pages of some high end catalogue. Although they held the same position his experience was evident, he effortlessly exuded a level of calm and confidence she could only dream of and with the designer clothes and obviously expensive watch he was the real deal.

He could see something was troubling her "Not long now." He said to fill the awkward silence whilst waiting for her to speak.

Justice

"No." She smiled and then looked down. She hadn't been aware that she was tapping her fingers on the desk until now. When she looked back up at Ishan she asked "Do you think it's strange that he was so compliant?"

"I think the whole thing is a bit strange to be honest, but picking him up today? No, not really. I think he's arrogant, he probably thinks he knows better than us, so he isn't worried. He's got to know we haven't got much on him, otherwise we would have brought him in before now." Ishan held her gaze before saying "We need to get him talking as soon as possible. I'll take the lead."

Claire was so relieved to hear that Ishan would be leading the interview. She'd never been involved in a case where they had so little evidence, where everything was riding on a confession of some kind and she was worried about how this could unfold. She was not naïve and had heard several stories of unscrupulous methods being used to 'grease the wheels' when a confession was essential, but she was suddenly nervous and the usual doubts about her own capabilities were starting to resurface. Before she could dwell any further on her own insecurities, Ishan gave her a reassuring smile and said "Come on then, let's do this, shall we?" as he picked up a leather-bound folder and headed towards the door.

Chapter 21

Ishan had gone in hard from the outset; Claire was surprised by just how hard. Although quite sparse, the interview room had the benefit of built in video and audio capability. She studied the suspect as Ishan spoke, clearly stating for the record, the names of those present and in what capacity they had come together in this stifling, windowless place. The young man raised his head for the first time when Ishan had said his name, Oliver James Jones, as he made eye contact he had quietly said "I prefer to be called Kelly."

"Well Oliver," he emphasised his name as he spoke "I would prefer it if I didn't have to speak to people like you about the death of a young girl, but there we are."

Claire watched as the small framed man lent forward, sliding his hands under his thighs, essentially reducing the space he occupied. He was wearing a navy blue sweatshirt and loose fitting jogging bottoms and despite his previous bravado, she could tell that having been left alone in the glaringly white, barren room, to consider his predicament had had a profound effect on him.

"So Oliver, how did you know Annabel McKenzie?" Ishan asked, aware that as he addressed him as Oliver he had visibly bristled. The silence hung in the air, before Ishan asked the question again.

Oliver appeared to be overwhelmed by the situation in which he had found himself, he was sweating, his skin visibly pale and clammy looking; his breathing was rapid and he was clearly distressed. Claire thought that perhaps he was unable to answer, that he was physically incapacitated by the enormity of the situation and the level of stress he was undoubtedly feeling. She was startled when Ishan banged his hand on to the table and once more asked "How did you know Annabel McKenzie?"

"She was my friend." the voice was small and insignificant, the non-verbal interaction virtually nil.

Justice

"Your friend?" Ishan scoffed, his voice raised "Your friend?" he twisted his neck to try and make eye contact, but all attempts were thwarted. "If she was your friend Oliver, how come her parents have never heard of you?" Ishan had recognised how uncomfortable he was with the name and secretly vowed to use it at every possibility in order to unsettle the young man.

"She was a fourteen year old girl Oliver, a fourteen year old girl that you had a secret relationship with for a very long time. A fourteen year old girl that you met, groomed and sexually assaulted isn't that the truth of the matter? Her parents knew nothing of you, because you made sure they didn't. You didn't want them to interfere, to prevent you from seeing your 'little orphan Annie' isn't that the truth?"

Oliver was suddenly transformed from a small, nervous, pathetic mass into a red faced vibrant creature, as with animal like speed he bounced from his seat shouting at the officer "You sick bastard, she was just a child!"

"Me? I'm the sick bastard?" Ishan raised his eyebrows and lowered his voice. "I haven't been meeting with a young girl behind her parents back, I haven't been sleeping with her and I didn't encourage her to end her life, just to get me off the hook when I'd had my fill, did I Oliver? That was you. All you Oliver." he slowly looked him up and down, taking in every inch of the man before him before continuing "What was it Oliver, she get to old for you?"

"How dare you? She was my friend, you ignorant bastard. She helped me. She was my friend!"

Claire had sat speechless for a moment as she had watched Oliver firstly sit back down and then slide to the floor. The large tears unashamedly ran down his face as he wrapped his arms around himself, rocking rhythmically, seeking any ounce of comfort he could find.

The interrogation had been relentless and Claire was willing it to end almost as much as their suspect.

Justice

"Bloody hell Ish." Was the sum total of her utterance as they had made their way up the stairs back to the office.

******

As they arrived they found Tommy stood at the green felt covered notice board, he was once again studying the sheets containing the text messages. "How's it going?" he asked not lifting his eyes from the numerous sheets of A4 paper.

"Not too bad, we've given him something's to think about and returned him to the cells. He should be ripe for the picking in about another hour or so." Ishan explained.

Tommy looked directly at an obviously mute Claire, before asking "You okay Claire?" to which she simply gave a quick nod of her head.

The tension within the office was suddenly shattered as they turned in unison to see an obviously jubilant Sergeant Slater making his way across the office. "Did you hear? Ten years! Ten bloody years!"

"Yes, well done Carl." Tommy was the first to congratulate the officer on his successful outcome in court "I hear it was a bit nip and tuck towards the end?"

"You could say that Boss, I was up against that new KC Lucas what's his name?"

"Williamson-Smyth." Claire offered.

"Yeah. That's him. Right tough nut that guy is." with hardly a pause he then asked "So what's going on here, we getting all cultured or something?" his eyes now looking beyond his colleagues were fixed firmly on the board.

"What do you mean?" Tommy asked; keen to gauge any views as to the elusive meaning of the texts.

Carl pointed seemingly randomly at one of the messages; they again acted as one, as they followed his finger.

May flights of angels sing thee to thy rest

Justice

They read the message once more, as they had read them all several times.

"These are the results of a message exchange found on the phone of Annabel McKenzie, some of them mention death, hence our interest." Tommy explained as he tapped the board with his index finger.

"No they don't reference death; well actually yes they do... but not really." Carl said as he continued to examine the board.

"What do you mean, Carl?" Tommy asked unable to hide the irritability in his voice.

"Yes, yes." he mumbled to himself in deep contemplation, refusing to be rushed as he scrutinised the messages pinned to the notice board, before confidently stating "These are all about suicide."

"What! Are you sure?" it was Tommy that asked the question, they were all thinking.

"Yes. This one," he replaced his finger and read aloud "'May fights of angels sing thee to thy rest' King Charles the third said this in his first televised speech as monarch, following the death of his mother the late Queen Elizabeth the second."

"But her death wasn't suicide." Ishan said oozing incredulity open mouthed and slack jawed at the preposterousness of the very suggestion.

"No, it wasn't." Carl replied "But before the good king said it, a certain Mr Bill Shakespeare had written a slightly longer version in Romeo and Juliet."

They looked at him stunned, only becoming more so as he casually added "You know 'goodnight sweet prince' and such."

The reference to a 'sweet prince' was not lost on any of them, they had seen the term of endearment scattered throughout the messages, this was what Annabel had called Oliver throughout their communications. The three were momentarily speechless.

Justice

"So, let me get this straight, these are all things William Shakespeare wrote?" Tommy could hardly breathe "And they're all about suicide?"

Carl looked intently at the board "Pretty much," he said "you've got Romeo and Juliet of course," he pointed to the verse that referred to kissing and explained "this is about the potential for Juliet to absorb any residue poison from the lips of Romeo," before seamlessly continuing "and there's some Antony and Cleopatra in there, along with some Hamlet and a little bit of Macbeth. It's not all Shakespeare though." he added "I don't recognise this here so I can't say for certain." he said as he indicated a small group of messages at the bottom of the third page, whilst the small group continued to follow his finger mesmerised "But all these others are definitely about suicide."

******

"Well, it's pretty cut and dry now isn't it?" Ishan was speaking a little while later, as the four sat huddled around his desk preparing their next plan of action.

"Seems so." Claire added, she was now feeling bad for the way she had been questioning Ishan's approach, after all, they had needed a confession. In fact they still needed a confession, but with Carl's unexpected input it was becoming clearer and clearer that Oliver had been openly discussing suicide with Annabel for a long time before her actual death, and along with the others, she had to agree there didn't seem to be any innocent reason for a grown man to be doing that.

"You okay Claire?" She was suddenly returned to the here and now by Tommy's voice. This was the second time since they had started the interview process he had asked how she was holding up and she was starting to be concerned he was having doubts about her ability. She gave what she thought was a positive smile as she replied "Of course Sir."

"So we're all agreed. We need to keep up the pressure and get a confession. We've got a lot riding on this." Tommy said summing up the plan they had been formulating.

Chapter 22

"So, Oliver. We know that you were meeting with Annabel, a fourteen year old child, at a place called the 'Edge' on a regular basis and we know that the main focus of your discussions when you met was suicide. We have the messages from Annabel's phone and we know that these messages are quotes from, in the main, Shakespearean plays or dramas as you will." He paused for dramatic effect, but his words appeared to go unheard. "So tell me Oliver, why would a grown man be so obsessed with discussing suicide with a child, a child that then goes on to commit suicide do you wonder?" Ishan asked in a quiet yet chillingly cold voice. When there was no reply he simply continued "You had been meeting Annabel in secret, you had been pretending to care for her..." This interrogation had been relentless for around 45 minutes during which time Oliver hadn't so much as made a murmur until now.

"I did care for her, I loved her, she was my friend." he stated quietly but emphatically.

"...having sex with her and then you played a part in killing her, isn't that what happened?" Ishan continued his sentence as if he hadn't heard him.

"You used her, you manipulated her and you are responsible for her death." Ishan was completely ruthless; Claire was speechless throughout, she had never seen him behave this way before. His manner irreconcilable with the warm, kind man she knew so well.

"She was my friend, she helped me. I loved her." His eyes were wet once again and he seemed to be less and less in control as Ishan continued, focused on his primary aim of obtaining a confession. "She was a beautiful young girl, her whole life ahead of her. Unfortunately she met you Oliver. You filled her head with thoughts of suicide and you and only you are solely

Justice

responsible for her death. Isn't that the absolute, undeniable truth Oliver?" he shouted

Oliver made a screech like a wounded animal before simply looking directly at Ishan and whispering just one word "Yes."

Claire watched in horror as the broken young man openly sobbed, making no attempt to wipe away the snot and tears that now poured from him as he confirmed over and over like a mantra, as if he was in some kind of trance "I'm sorry, I'm responsible for her death."

As they ascended the staircase once more, Claire was in turmoil, they had left Oliver 'to sweat' again having made a break through, but she was ill at ease about the ferocity of their approach and her involvement with it. She had never been involved in a case like this, where they were relying on self-incrimination by the suspect and found herself waging an internal battle, with a mixture of emotions as she sat down quietly at her desk.

S. J. McDonald

After making a cup of camomile tea that she hadn't drunk and poking around in a box of Tesco prawn salad her usual doubts returned with a vengeance and she contemplated once again if she really had what it takes to be an effective police officer. She knew she could never have 'switched it on' as the ever restrained, calm and calculated Ishan had today and she felt sympathy for the young man currently 'sweating' downstairs, undoubtedly dreading round three. Her thoughts were interrupted when a young duty officer she knew only as 'Dave from the interview suite' popped his head through the doorway to announce, "There's a solicitor here for Oliver Jones, so give me a call before you come back down, as they're currently having a tête-à- tête."

Claire couldn't help feeling a little relieved as she promptly walked to Tommy's office where he and Ishan were currently entrenched, no doubt discussing strategy, to impart the latest news from 'Dave from the interview suite'.

Chapter 23

It was a further hour until they were again descending the stairs to the interview suite, following notification from the ever nondescript Dave that Oliver and his Solicitor were in room four and ready to proceed. Their footsteps were the only audible sound, as they made their way back to the interview suite, both deep in their own thoughts.

As they entered the room Claire was immediately hit by the appearance of Oliver, his tired red eyes gave no indication that he had even registered their presence; his previously slight frame appeared to have diminished even further and his posture could be likened to that of a jellyfish, devoid of all structure or support. In direct contrast the gentleman sat next to him was ramrod straight, his expensive, made to measure suit hung naturally on his tanned, chiselled body. He was a handsome man, with a symmetrical face and piercing green eyes and Claire got the impression he was fully aware of how attractive he was. He stood to greet them and offered a firm, no nonsense handshake. His voice was soft and smooth and had a tangible warmth to it, Claire could image him reading to a small child, and yet she acknowledged as he spoke there were clear undertones of confidence, precision and power. He had introduced himself as 'Theodore Masterson' and Claire couldn't help thinking his name really suited him; it too was strong and uncompromising.

They had no sooner sat than he asked "Can you tell me why my client did not have a solicitor present during his..." he made a display of his slight but derisory cough, before sarcastically completing his sentence "...interview?" If the words had left any doubt at all, the way he looked at both Ishan and Claire clarified his feelings of unadulterated contempt.

Ishan was clearly caught off guard from the start "I can assure you that Mr Jones was informed of his rights from the outset," Claire had to agree, he had been told

Justice

he could have a solicitor present, "and he has been afforded the necessary respect and courtesy throughout this process." Claire silently hoped that she would never be called upon to corroborate this particular statement.

The level of disdain was palpable and Claire wished she could simply disappear as the lawyer scornfully continued. "I would like to read a statement prepared on behalf of my client, after which he will gladly answer any and all outstanding questions you may have." For the next fifteen minutes the officers sat in abject silence as they listened to Theodore Masterson unveiling the details within the statement one by one, as if he were leading them naturally towards the climax of a well written novel. Concluding with the sentence "and therefore I expect my client to be released, without prejudice, with immediate effect."

A thousand questions raced through Ishan's mind, but it was Claire who spoke, gently, addressing her question directly at Oliver "So why did you tell us that you were responsible for her death?" She watched as the now shattered young man simply replied "Because I am." He turned his bloodshot eyes towards hers as he explained "I should have known she was unhappy, I should have prevented this from happening." He swallowed hard, as if he had a lump of concrete wedged in his throat, before saying. "I loved her, she was my only friend. The only person that ever helped me." The pain was clearly etched on his face as he continued "But she was young and I shouldn't have spoken to her the way I did, I never thought she would do anything to harm herself." He stopped for a second trying to compose himself as he wiped his tear-stained face with the back of his hand. "I was selfish, wrapped up in my own problems, she was never meant to die." His eyes locked firmly on Claire's, almost pleading for her understanding as he stated "The only person that was supposed to die was Oliver James Jones." The misery in his voice, in his guilt wracked body was painful to watch, but Claire found it difficult to look

Justice

away as Oliver collapsed in upon himself once more, devastated by the result of his own actions.

Chapter 24

The team had all gathered around to hear Ishan definitively explain why they had had no choice but to cut Oliver loose. He had already agreed with Tommy to start at the beginning 'warts and all' and so he now stood, slightly to the left of the notice board, which exposed the woefully inadequate information they had amassed so far, to begin. "Right guys. So it seems that Oliver met Annabel when she attended a local theatre group to try out for the part of Juliet in an up-coming production of Romeo and Juliet."

"Her parents never mentioned she was involved in amateur dramatics did they?" Tim asked immediately, unsettling Ishan before he could get into his stride.

If Tim had waited just a moment I would have covered this Ishan thought, a discernable tone of irritation evident in his voice as he continued. "No they didn't Tim, because they didn't know. Apparently it was a one time thing and Annabel didn't get the part, I assume if

Justice

she had been successful, she would have been forced to tell her parents about it. According to Oliver she had said they wouldn't have approved, seems they were keen that she spent her time on more academic studies."

Ishan took an extended breath "Anyway, it was here that she met Oliver who was involved in scenery design, painting backgrounds and the like. Apparently, despite the age difference, they hit it off instantly, becoming firm friends straight away. Claire you pointed out a while back that Annabel wouldn't just befriend a male adult, because of the inherent potential dangers, but Annabel recognised early doors that Oliver didn't pose a danger to her."

"He's gay?" Tim asked.

"No he, err. He's not gay, but neither did he have any sexual intent towards her. He didn't want to hurt Annabel, if anything he wanted to be her."

"What do you mean?" Carl asked "He wanted to be a young girl?"

"Yes, well, no, more precisely he wanted to become a woman Carl." Ishan explained "Oliver had been confused about his sexuality for some time. But forming a close friendship with and speaking to Annabel he had finally come to a decision that he wanted to end the life he knew as Oliver and start a new life as Kelly. By the way, this name was in reference to his idol, the film actress come princess, Grace Kelly and not as previously thought, by some of the local Neanderthals, in homage to a serial killing cannibal. Hence all the cryptic talk of suicide within their text messages.

"I don't get it, if he wanted to live as a woman, why didn't he just get on and do it? That's fairly common place in today's society, there's no real judgement on alternative lifestyles these days." Tim asked.

"If only that were true, Tim." Tommy looked genuinely remorseful as he continued to explain "After meeting

Justice

his mother I can easily foresee the difficulties Oliver must have had to endure in his attempt to put his previous life to bed and move forward as he desired to live. People can be so cruel," he paused before adding "seems our girl really was a beautiful soul, simply accepting Oliver for who he was and wanting to help him overcome the obstacles he was experiencing in trying to become Kelly, it's as simple as that."

"So he's transgender, and they used to meet at the 'edge' and discuss him transitioning? That's it?" Carl asked, again somewhat disappointed.

"Well, I'm sure they discussed more than that Carl." Ishan said "And it turns out that the edge wasn't a real place, it was apparently a reference to D.H.Lawrence."

"Of course." Carl said, "It's about seeing things differently, viewing life differently" he continued, reciting for the benefit of his colleagues "Life is a travelling to the edge of knowledge, then a leap taken."

Tommy's eyebrows were raised once more at the unexpected wealth of knowledge Carl seemed to possess.

"So where does all this leave us now boss?" Tim asked.

Tommy summed up their current position "Well, we now have precisely nothing. No leads. No insight as to what may have happened to Annabel. No idea even if a crime has actually been committed. Nothing, zero, nada, jack shit, as they say." He chewed on the inside of his cheek as he considered with some dread, having to explain to Stephenson that he had in fact backed the wrong horse.

******

"Dickie's not going to be happy." Ishan stated the obvious, after the team had started to disperse.

"No. He most certainly is not Ishan and a word of warning, if DCI Stephenson ever catches you calling him Dickie he'll have your guts for garters."

Justice

"What you going to do?"

"Tonight? Nothing. We've got Annabel's funeral tomorrow morning, this will all keep until after that. Let's go home. As they say 'tomorrow is another day'."

On the drive home Ishan couldn't keep his mind focused on any one thing. He was worried about Tommy, he looked permanently tired, his grey hair had lost its lustre, his skin was dull and his eyes seemed eternally world weary. He indicated to turn right at the traffic lights and as he sat waiting for the green light to shine, his thoughts also changed direction. He had been so hard on Oliver, a young man in turmoil, who already had so many challenges to overcome in life, he felt wracked with guilt for adding to the weight of an already heavy burden. He was ashamed of the way he had behaved today, so desperate for that elusive confession; he knew it would be a long time, if ever, before his previously good relationship with Claire would be restored. And what of Annabel, they had failed her. They knew no more now than the day she died. He suddenly became aware of the sound of a car horn and saw that the lights were green, before he could react a rather large SUV drove around him, the driver shouting obscenities and as Ishan saw the drivers blurred, none too subtle hand gesture, he realised he was weeping.

Much later, when he finally climbed into bed next to his steadfast, loving partner, hearing the usual, yet comforting words "You alright love?" He had simply replied "Bad day at the office." before allowing himself to be comforted, held and cradled like a baby.

Chapter 25

Ishan and Tommy had attended many funerals in a formal capacity, too many to count. The process for them was usually an opportunity to study the bereaved in attendance, to scrutinise the congregation identifying anyone behaving strange, out of the ordinary. Today however, was different. There would be no shady characters hiding in the crowd, no unexpected figures trying to blend in or dark silhouettes milling around at the back of the church. They didn't expect a break in the case, they were purely here to show their support to the family and pay their respects to a young girl whose life force had been snuffed out far too soon, like a candle in an unforeseeable gust.

Father Mark had performed an upbeat ceremony, a fitting celebration of Annabel's short life. The church was filled with fresh flowers and Tommy wondered when he had last attended a funeral so colourful, he knew only too well that it was normal practice these days to limit flowers, encouraging would be senders to instead provide monetary donations to a worthwhile charity. Tommy considered this fact for a moment, was it because the deceased where usually older, more sensible and set in their ways, wishing to use valuable resources wisely. Was the church simply filled with colourful flowers today because Annabel had not lived long enough to become sensible and rigid in her thinking? Was she still in effect a frivolous, light hearted young girl? Was that how her loved ones would see her in their minds eye forever? He pondered, as he now sees Cathy, frozen in time, in virtual suspended animation. Or would they torture themselves with questions of who she would have become, a wife, a mother and what she could have achieved had she lived.

"What do you think?

He suddenly realised Ishan was speaking to him "Sorry, what's that?" he asked.

Justice

"I said do you think we should take another run at the father?" Ishan whispered again furtively to avoid being overheard.

"I don't know, what do you think?" Tommy replied solemnly.

The question remained unanswered as they turned in harmony to see Mr and Mrs McKenzie and their remaining child leading the funeral cortege, walking towards them, following an impossibly small coffin on its final short journey.

******

"You will come back for some food won't you Inspector?" Mrs McKenzie asked as they stood in the bright sunshine. The interment had been a quick but definitive act, decisively concluding the life of her daughter.

"Thank you, that's very kind. But we won't if you don't mind. Things to do," he gave a weak, sombre smile as he went on to say "we will, however, need to call by tomorrow if that's okay?"

"Yes of course." She replied, as she blended into a small crowd of well-wishers comprising of extended family members, friends, neighbours and a contingent of both pupils and teachers from St Edmunds.

As they watched the various groups of mourners meander their way through the churchyard, no doubt each consumed by their own private thoughts Ishan turned to Tommy. "She's a remarkable women, isn't she Tommy?" He commented "The more we see of her the more impressed I am. If I had lost a child I don't think I would be able to cope getting out of bed in the morning never mind much else, I don't think I'd ever get over it."

"I don't think you can ever get over something so devastating. It's utterly tragic to lose a child, but you're right about one thing Ishan, she's been astonishingly strong and so incredibly dignified from the start." he observed.

Justice

"Should we take another look at the father?" Ishan repeated his earlier question with little enthusiasm.

"We can I suppose, but we have absolutely nothing on him and in all honesty, I don't fancy him for any involvement at any stage, do you really?" He looked miserable as he took in the meticulously maintained grounds "No. I just feel that if he had posed any kind of threat to her children Sandy McKenzie would have already addressed it, husband or not, don't you?"

"Yeah, I suppose so."

They walked in silence towards the car. Both agonisingly aware, that when they met with Annabel's parents the following day, barring a miracle, they would have no answers for them.

Chapter 26

"Can I have a word Sir?" Claire had wasted no time in approaching Tommy and Ishan as they arrived in the office. She appeared anxious, her posture and expression screaming concern and there was a slight tremor of panic to her voice as she spoke.

"Yes, of course, what is it?"

"No Sir. In private." she indicated his office with an almost imperceptible gesture of her head.

Tommy stopped in his tracks as he started to explain "No problem, I'm in with the Chief in about an hour and I'm just about to grab some lunch. Can it wait until this afternoon?"

"No Sir, I don't think it can." was her distinctly shaky reply, "Probably best you hear this before your meeting with the Chief."

Justice

They walked towards Tommy's office, leaving Ishan open mouthed, agog, lost in his thoughts - surely Claire wasn't going to report him for his handling of Oliver the previous day, was she? Yes he had been assertive, forceful even, but they had needed a confession, he reasoned with himself, justifying the actions and approach he had taken. He was frozen to the spot, unable to move, paralysed with fear, as he recalled how she had told Tommy she needed to speak with him before his weekly scheduled meeting with Stephenson, so he deduced if this was about him, this was going to be serious.

******

They had entered the office and were now sat facing one another on either side of the larger than average desk, that always looked out of place in the smaller than average office. Tommy looked meaningfully at Claire willing her to speak.

After a short while, she had clearly garnered the strength to do so as she started "Do you remember when you first came back to work Sir?"

"Yes." he replied, watching her intently, wondering where this was going.

"Well, do you remember that after a couple of weeks you were the designated senior officer on call at the weekend for the region?"

"Yes, I remember that Claire." she was clearly struggling to get to the point.

"Do you recall that that was the on call duty when Annabel McKenzie died?"

"Yes I remember that weekend Claire."

"Well you will recall it was a very busy weekend for us." She was fidgeting with the skin on her thumb and avoiding eye contact.

"Bloody hell, for god's sake Claire, what is this? Do you have something to tell me or did you just fancy giving

Justice

me some sort of memory test. You worried I could have developed Alzheimer's disease or something." He was hungry and frustrated and it showed.

"Sorry boss." She mumbled her voice little more than a squeak, as she continued to look at the desk whilst violently assaulting the skin around her thumbnail. Tommy was immediately sorry for the way he'd spoken to her. She was obviously concerned about something.

"Okay, let's start at the beginning, shall we?" he asked in his more familiar reassuring tone. "It was a busy weekend." She raised her head and looked him in the eye as he continued "So what do you want to tell me?" he asked, he hadn't, however, been prepared for the answer she provided.

As he sat and listened intently, all he could think was that Stephenson would hand him his arse on a platter over this one.

******

Ishan had been sat at his desk reliving every encounter he had had with their suspect the previous day and dreading what was to come, when Claire had rushed past his desk and out the office door towards the ladies toilets. She hadn't made any attempt to engage with him and she seemed upset. Suddenly he was sure of what she had done, she had reported him for his aggressive behaviour, a rush of anxiety consumed him and he was distraught, this was it. In one foul swoop this was the end of his career, his future, his life as he knew it he thought. He wondered how he would be able to break the news to Em that he was going to be kicked out of the force, that he wasn't the man he appeared to be. He wondered too how he would deal with the shame about to be dropped on him from a great height. He knew from previous cases that these types of complaints dragged on for an age, but the stigma never, ever went away.

"Ishan, do you have a moment?" Tommy's voice prevented him from pulling his mind and body together,

Justice

his legs felt wobbly and disconnected as he stood silently and followed Tommy to the his office.

Once sat down Tommy had wasted no time at all explaining what Claire had said to him. Ishan found it hard to follow the conversation as his mind was contending with a myriad of raw emotions ranging from initial dread to an overwhelming relief, along with an inescapable guilt, he knew only too well he had sailed too close to the wind with his interrogation methods and as such deserved everything he got, he also made himself a solemn promise that if he escaped judgement today with his career and reputation intact he would never overstep the mark like that again.

"So, what do you think?" Tommy had mistakenly taken Ishan's silence and serious expression for attention and understanding. Ishan chastised himself internally for his vivid imagination before he spoke.

"It's certainly a head scratcher boss."

"'It's a head scratcher?' that's your considered opinion is it Sergeant, good job I called you in then isn't it? What, with insight like that I'd better watch out, you could be head hunted to run Scotland Yard any bloody day now, and where would that leave me?"

"Sorry Sir." he stammered "I'm feeling a bit off, what with the funeral and missing lunch and everything."

Tommy looked at the younger man, compassion in his eyes, yesterday's disappointments had obviously hit him harder than he had realised, and he knew only too well, that like himself, Ishan functioned best on a fully belly.

"Okay then, once again, the highlights only this time, try and keep up". His eyes were locked on Ishan's as he started to relay the details once more. "Claire has been contacted by another team; they wanted to inform her that there had been a DA resulting in death involving one of our previous cases."

Justice

This in itself was not unusual, Ishan thought, in fact sharing relevant information was considered best practice in terms of increasing overall knowledge, encouraging replication of successful and effective policing methods and providing learning opportunities where things hadn't gone well.

"You'll remember a little while back, on our last on call together we got a shout to an address on 'Millionaires row'." The epitaph was well known and frequently used to denote one of the roughest parts of Manchester "A Mr and Mrs Mazur."

"Yes, of course. The shovel thing and she's killed him this time, has she?" Ishan asked

"No, he's killed her." Tommy's voice was serious, his complexion sallow

"I'm sorry sir, I'm not getting it. Sad as these things are, it's not uncommon for domestic abuse to escalate into homicide, why does this concern us?" he asked.

"It concerns us because when we were involved. Mrs Mazur had hit Mr Mazur on the back of the head with a garden spade. And when I asked Claire about any previous history of domestic abuse she reported, via Tim, that there wasn't any."

"Okay...?"

"But it transpires that Tim had only done a search against the wife and the current address for call outs. Completely missing that the husband had a sheet of offences as long as my arm."

"So...?" The enormity of what he was hearing suddenly hit him.

"Yes Ishan. This poor woman was left with no follow up, no welfare visits, no referrals to other agencies that could have provided her with help and support. She was just left to get on with it!"

Ishan cursed under his breath "How could that happen?"

Justice

"Well, if you mull that over for an hour or so, you'll be where I am, still bloody clueless." Tommy replied adding, "The incident we attended could well have been her first and last attempt at protecting herself or of trying to escape him. Who knows what he would have put her through once he was discharged from hospital?" Tommy's lips were almost invisible as he sucked them between his teeth.

"What will you tell Stephenson?"

"Everything." Was the blunt reply "I called his PA earlier to say I couldn't make the regular appointment, it's being rearranged for later today."

"What do you think will happen to Claire?" Ishan's unease clearly discernable.

"Honestly, I don't know. Dickie is unpredictable at the best of times; I would imagine at the very least we are looking at her getting a suspension whilst there's an internal investigation."

Neither spoke for a long time until Tommy asked "You hungry?" to which Ishan responded with a miserable look and a simple shake of the head.

"No, me neither."

Chapter 27

Weekly meetings with the Detective Chief Inspector seemed to come around at an ever increasing pace. Tommy fully understood he was obliged to meet with his superior to provide updates on the progress of on-going cases and as a means of having his personal performance monitored. He had never actually bothered to read it, but he assumed that the HR handbook would probably describe these meetings as 'a two way street, where both parties could contribute ideas, seeking positive solutions to any issues or problems that may exist, in a supportive and non-judgemental environment'. That certainly wasn't his experience. He'd been attending this weekly charade for the last eighteen months now, ever since Richard Stephenson had been promoted to a position he was clearly over qualified for and under experienced to perform.

S. J. McDonald

There had been a mutual disliking from the outset, when Stephenson had announced at his first meeting with staff that he had been appointed to improve performance, referring to himself menacingly as a 'new brush, not afraid to sweep clean.' In a very long and instantly forgettable speech he had talked of uniting the staff and in fairness he had, there was a universal hatred for the man, due to his patronising attitude towards senior officers and downright rudeness to everyone else.

The role of the DCI was supposed to be hands on, but Tommy had never really witnessed Stephenson in action, moreover he interfered with operations, wanting to know all the details without doing any of the work. Stephenson was a political beast, he had made it clear this role was merely a necessary step on his journey to much higher and better things, that he was destined for greatness and as such he had somehow managed to ensconce himself in an office on the management floor, at the top of the four story building.

Justice

As he sat in the plush surroundings of the management suite reception, Tommy deliberated how, no matter what time his appointment was; he was always expected to sit in the waiting room with the ever inhospitable PA, Margery.

When the unnecessary mind games came to an end, the sour faced Margery turned towards him and pursed her lips before stating, "You may now go in." As he stood he made a conscious effort not to indulge her with any kind of acknowledgment or thank you.

Despite having been kept waiting for eighteen minutes, he was unsurprised as he entered the spacious office to be greeted only with a view of the top of the senior officer's balding head, as he scribbled notes, using an impressive Montblanc pen, as if his very life depended upon it.

After an inordinate amount of time passed Tommy made a show of slowly lifting his jacket and shirt sleeves with his index finger in order to view his shabby old watch with its well-worn black leather strap. The stand-off however, continued, even though both were fully aware that Stephenson had seen him, none too subtly check the time. Tommy could feel his blood boiling as he studied the arrogant little man sat behind his enormous, highly polished walnut desk.

Suddenly following an extravagant display of putting the top on his gold designer ink pen he finally spoke "Ah. Marsden. There you are."

"Yes sir, here I am." was Tommy's clipped response. He wanted to add "you time wasting, egotistical, supercilious bastard" but instead simply afforded the man a contemptuous smile. How he hated the air of pretence that surrounded this patronising idiot.

"Please Thomas, do sit down." he stood slightly, extending a scrawny arm to indicate the chair.

"Thank you sir." Tommy replied through clenched teeth.

Justice

Both men looked directly at the other as the senior office finally said "Good that you could make it after all." the hostility of the seemingly innocuous words was not lost on Tommy.

"Yes, I'm sorry about the need to rearrange, unfortunately something cropped up." Tommy said, clearing his throat.

"Well let's start with that then, shall we?"

Over the next five minutes Tommy laid bare the facts surrounding the domestic abuse case involving Mr and Mrs Mazur. Explaining how Claire's negligence had resulted in a level of inaction that in turn, may very well have contributed to the death of the long suffering wife.

Stephenson's head had been moving slowly, rhythmically whilst Tommy had spoken, he was quiet for a moment before asking "So what, if anything do you want to do?"

"Well, I think we need to know exactly what happened." Tommy replied a little surprised by the question.

"Haven't you just told me what happened? Sergeant Johnson was careless with regards to police procedure. But you know as well as I do how these things go," he waited a second before continuing, a look on his face that Tommy thought was supposed to convey a degree of remorse "if we had known that Mr Mazur was a violent repeat offender it would probably have made no difference whatsoever to the eventual outcome. These women never leave, they just continue the cycle." he said.

Tommy was incredulous, finding it hard to believe Stephenson was actually saying these words; his shock was further enhanced when he had then added "And of course the cost to the service, of continually going out, every time there's a slight disagreement and a bit of a tussle is absolutely phenomenal."

Justice

Tommy was stunned, totally speechless as he scrutinised the man, eventually he managed a simple muttering "But, a woman has been killed Sir!"

"Yes and that's sad of course, but as with all these things it's only ever a question of time." he fixed his gaze squarely on Tommy's face as he said "No point rocking the boat." with that the conversation was over as far as the Detective Chief Inspector was concerned.

Tommy was dumbfounded; he didn't know what to think as he asked "So what should I do with Claire?" he had expected the answer to involve retraining, maybe a disciplinary and perhaps a written warning of sorts. What he didn't expect was what he got! Stephenson had simply informed him that in his opinion there was no point in taking the matter any further. Tommy didn't think he could be more shocked by the cavalier attitude of his boss, but he was totally flabbergasted when he'd explained that it would just be an unnecessary waste of time, money and effort, investing valuable resources, given Claire's age.

S. J. McDonald

When Tommy had said he didn't follow, it seems that his boss believed that a rising of the eyebrows whilst articulating a single word "babies." required no additional explanation.

Chapter 28

By the time Tommy closed the office door behind him he was astounded, confused and horrified by the entire encounter. He was not the most PC man alive; he knew that only too well, he had had countless struggles with what he should and shouldn't say and do, in what he considered to be the ever changing mine field of political correctness. But despite his occasional clumsiness in choosing the right words, he had always tried to treat everyone equally, respectfully. Never wanting to hurt or offend anyone else, demonstrating an acceptance of everyone that was how he was, how he had always been, how he'd been raised.

With no real recollection of the journey from the top floor he found himself entering a dimly lit office space stupefied. He made his way through the empty space, retrieving his jacket from the old coat stand in the corner of his tiny office when he suddenly heard a familiar voice "You okay Tom?" He turned to see Ishan at the far end of the room. Concern emblazoned across this face, detracting from his usual natural appeal.

"Thought I was alone." he mumbled in reply.

"Loo." Ishan said, his thumb indicating over his left shoulder in the general direction of the toilets as way of an explanation. He stood silent for a moment, drinking in a dazed looking Tommy before asking again if he was alright.

"Yes, I'm fine." he said attempting to wave away Ishan's fretfulness with his hand.

"Pub?" Ishan glumly proposed

"Um…Err yes… why not."

The cold night air was biting at their hands and seeping through the soles of their shoes as they scurried towards their familiar sanctuary.

Justice

By the time they entered The Three Bells and found a quiet table away from other customers Tommy was feeling less stunned and increasingly angry following his meeting with the Detective Chief Inspector.

"So what's going to happen to Claire?" Ishan wasted no time, his fear for his friend and colleague clearly visible in the well lit room, his anxiety made more obvious in the glow of the warm coal fire.

"Well, apparently nothing." Tommy said in an angry, scathing tone. "Apparently Mrs Mazur was always destined to die at the hands of her violent bully husband and apparently Claire's career will be over soon enough when she decides to stop pretending to be a copper and gets on with her true vocation of being a bloody mother." Tommy was talking quietly to prevent being overheard, but there was no disguising the venom dripping from his tongue.

Ishan's expression conveyed shock and bewilderment as he stared intently and quietly asked "My god, what the hell happened?" Tommy spent twenty minutes recalling the conversation about the Mazur's. Ishan had never seen Tommy so enraged, at times spittle was being expelled along with the disgusting words from his mouth as Ishan sat stunned and amazed finally asking "How the hell can he behave like that?"

Tommy shook his head in bewilderment, before remorsefully adding. "I don't know Ish; I have never heard such blatant and aggressive misogyny in my entire life. And when I tried to get him to see reason, he started preaching about how the police are allowed to do their jobs via mutual consent with the public, how recent high profile criminal cases involving serving offices had dented confidence in the police and how we shouldn't create unnecessary problems by highlighting simple acts of procedural carelessness. 'Unnecessary problems', I ask you...Really! A woman has died for god's sake and he's likening it to someone having filled in the wrong bloody form!" Tommy was once again incandescent with rage.

Justice

Ishan was still silent, looking completely bemused when Tommy added, as if as an afterthought "Oh and the McKenzie case is being shelved. I can't tell you how much pain I got for that, wasting time, money and effort and for bringing Oliver in. Apparently that doesn't look good on us at all!"

Tommy looked away for a second to compose himself before saying "Obviously we should have known that he was struggling, poor kid; known that he could have been suffering as a result of transgender issues and experiences, and questioning him, given the outcome, could be perceived as discriminatory. You know how it's all about the optics these days." Tommy gave a slight humourless laugh as he said "The irony of the lecture Dickie gave me about treating everyone equally and respectfully was not lost on me, given his distorted view of the world and women in particular, I can tell you that!" Tommy sucked his lips in so hard they almost disappeared before saying "What a totally horrible and wicked world we live in Ish. Where a young person isn't allowed to live as they would want to, and their only support is a young girl. It makes you think doesn't it?"

Ishan had stayed late because he had wanted to speak with Tommy. To tell him that he was feeling bad about the way the interview with Oliver had gone, but he recognised tonight was not the time to add to his friend's frustrations. Tonight it seemed they had both wordlessly agreed was a time for drowning their sorrows.

"Same again?" Tommy asked, picking up their empty glasses.

It was going to be a long night, Ishan gave a lacklustre smile. "Yeah, why not?"

Chapter 29

"What the...No!" Tommy cursed under his breath; surely it couldn't be morning already. The cruelty of the screeching alarm clock was relentless, and as he made his third attempt to silence it, he was seriously contemplating throwing it against the bedroom wall. He was already late for work, but as he fell back on to his pillows he could not have cared less. His head hurt and his bloodshot eyes stung when he tried to open them, the sun streaming through the still open curtains was uncompromising, he turned his body, seeking solace under the duvet, to avoid the stark brightness that harshly filled the room. His recollections of the previous night were patchy to say the least, but he did recall Bill joining Ishan and himself in a 'few drinks' after the pub doors were closed and Ada had taken herself off to bed. The kindly landlord had produced what he had referred to as the 'good stuff' and the trio had carried on drinking until their respective problems had melted away like a child's snowman in the light of a new day.

He was comfortable, returning to his slumber, with the duvet firmly over his head when the noise started to pierce his brain again. He stuck his arm out of the simulated darkness and reached for the clock, discovering it was no longer the offending article. Suddenly silence. "Thank god" he mumbled, just as the interruption restarted like a pneumatic drill at the end of the bed.

It took all his energy to rummage around in the pile of clothes he found casually strewn around the bedroom floor before he finally retrieved his work phone.

"Morning Sir." he struggled for a minute to place the cheery, almost mocking voice.

"Yes, good morning Carl. How can I help you?" Tommy cleared his dry throat. The pretence of professionalism was fooling no one, especially himself.

Justice

"Thing is, it's nine forty five boss and... well I noticed that both yours and Ishan's cars were still in the car park, so I assume you were busy last night. Thought, perhaps you would like a lift in today."

"Yes, thanks Carl that would be very helpful." Tommy said trying to maintain an air of civility. It felt like his head would split open, spewing the contents of his skull all over the beige carpet at any minute. His nausea subsided as all he could think about was the predicament he was in and that of all the possible people it could have been; it had to be Carl to phone him.

"Okay, I'll pick you up and then swing by for Ishan and Claire on the way back."

The mention of Claire's name sent a panic through him. He had sent her home yesterday and told her to stay there until she was contacted. Trying to save some semblance of authority he said "That's great Carl, but Claire can make her own way in; just ask Julie to call her and ask her to be in my office by twelve thirty would you?"

"Will do, I should be at yours in about forty minutes, traffic depending."

Tommy collapsed back on the bed still holding the phone to his ear; he had forty minutes to make a 'silk purse out of a sow's ear' as his grandma had frequently said, it would be a very tall order indeed.

******

Carl arrived and knocked on the glass panel in the front door dead on time. Tommy was still struggling to fasten his tie, when he reached over and flicked the catch to allow Carl a view of the hallway, but nothing else. He was grumbling internally about Carl's seemingly newfound respect for punctuality. "Morning Carl thanks for the lift." Was all he said as he pulled the door shut and walked down the empty driveway.

"No problem boss, we're a team after all." he said without the vaguest hint of sarcasm.

Justice

As Tommy climbed into the passenger seat he was handed a packet of extra strong mints, he popped one into his mouth and took a long look at the younger man pulling at his seatbelt. He'd never really taken the time to get to know him and he suddenly felt a wave of shame wash over him.

After a moment Tommy asked "So Carl, how are you finding it in the team, settling in with everyone are you?" He was still feeling rough; there was only so much two Paracetamols could do for you, but as they were in a confined space it seemed like the polite thing to do.

"I pretty much keep myself to myself really," Carl said as he navigated a large roundabout, "you know what it's like when you move teams under difficult circumstances. No one wants to get too close. You know, in case you rat them out for something." He glanced over at Tommy, a slight smile playing at the edge of his lips momentarily "Unclean. Just short of the bell!" He said whilst giving a quick mirthless laugh.

Tommy hadn't known the reason for Carls transfer at short notice, only that it was happening. He had presumed that it was a case of moving a problem; it wasn't unheard of that poorly performing officers with bad attitudes were moved from team to team as an alternative to incompetent seniors addressing their issues. At the time Cathy had been ill and his priorities elsewhere, now he wondered if he had assumed too much. In fairness he thought, Carl had made no attempts to integrate with the others, but was that because of him or them he now wondered. Carl's conversation seemed to suggest he had been a whistle blower of some sorts, which, if true would be news to him. Tommy gave a rueful smile and decided to quickly change the subject, whilst silently vowing to get to the bottom of Carl's transfer. "So, tell me Carl, how'd you know so much about Shakespearian play writes and things?" he asked.

"Honestly?"

"Yes please." Tommy replied.

Justice

By the time they pulled up in front of the impressive city centre apartments which Ishan called home Tommy was mesmerised by the breadth and depth of Carl's knowledge. As the son of a barrister he had attended the prestigious Manchester Grammar School for boys, from the age of seven until he was eighteen, where he'd acquired not only the ability to recite plays by Shakespeare, and poetry from Byron, Keats and many others off pat, but had also become fluent in four languages and played the violin badly. Despite briefly outlining a number of impressive achievements during their short discussion Tommy got the impression the younger man was being quite modest about his accomplishments.

"Morning." Ishan said as he climbed into the back of Carl's silver, no frills people carrier, moving a colourful rag doll into a child's car seat situated to his right. "Thanks for the lift Carl, appreciated."

"No problem." he replied.

Tommy studied Carl for a brief moment as he struggled to find a gap in the traffic, he seemed genuinely happy to be helping out his colleagues, being part of something. As he eventually pulled out into the flow of traffic Tommy was deep in thought, could it be possible that the entire team had treated Carl incredibly badly he mused, if that was the case he knew they had been following his lead, he instantly felt the heat radiating from his face, his embarrassment adding to his overall feelings of discomfort.

Chapter 30

It was already a difficult day; there was a tangible listlessness throughout the office, a collective apathy. It was understandable given the disappointing direction the McKenzie case had taken. Tommy sat behind his desk nursing his aching head. Ishan, he'd noticed, was faring much better than himself. Was that an age thing he wondered, feeling so very old all of a sudden?

He fixated on the wall clock; the minute hand seemed to be as energetic as he felt. It was twelve twenty four and he instinctively knew Claire would be dead on time. He had spent a while deliberating on how to deal with her, continually questioning what he should say to her about the Mazur case.

******

Claire had arrived in the car park a few minutes after noon. As she'd sat in her car awaiting her appointment with Tommy, she was feeling queasy, her palms felt clammy, her mind in turmoil. Following a sleepless night she was surprisingly alert. She checked her watch again and sighed, reapplied the soft peach lipstick she usually only wore for interviews, family dinners or special occasions and checked her face in a silver compact mirror.

She was anxious about her meeting with Tommy, but the overwhelming emotion coursing through her body was unquestionably one of anger. She was angry at Tim for making such a stupid mistake, angry at herself for not having supervised him correctly, not having realised what he'd done, but mostly she was angry that when he came to her flat last night, when she most needed comfort, support and understanding, his primary and only concern was for himself and how this could possibly affect him; his career!

She recalled now as she adjusted her pantsuit jacket, how as soon as she'd answered the door the first words out of his mouth were to ask if she had mentioned his name to Tommy when they had spoken. His utter

Justice

selfishness and total disregard for her feelings had been an epiphany; like a long line of men, he'd made a fool of her and she'd been stupid enough to let him, what had she been thinking? When would she ever learn? She was so angry with herself, but she was bloody furious with Tim.

******

Tommy watched now as Claire quietly walked through the open plan office, and exactly as predicted, she gently tapped on the glass panel of his small office door at precisely twelve thirty.

Chapter 31

"Ishan are you ready? We can go in two cars and then I'm off home to bed. I feel awful" Tommy said furtively. Ishan collected his belongings, hot on the tail of his superior. As he passed Claire's desk he'd studied the ground as he walked, not knowing what he should or could say to the sad young woman sat at her desk, eyes glued to her computer screen to avoid any form of interaction.

Once alone in the car Tommy reached into the glove compartment to retrieve some more Paracetamol in an attempt to dull the pain in his head, but his conscience would not be silenced. He reflected now on his conversation with Claire; how he had focused his energy on explaining that Mrs Mazur had been spoken to numerous times, given encouragement and offered support to facilitate her leaving her husband. He had emphasised that frequently her injuries had been so severe she had required hospitalisation, yet she

Justice

consistently refused to end the abusive relationship. He highlighted how she had remained silent during their involvement with her, not once alerting the officers to her plight, which he said was a clear indication that she would prefer to remain within the toxic environment. And he had stated that given these undisputed facts he had decided to use this as a learning experience for her, reiterating several times the importance of following correct procedures and stressing that there must be no recurrence of this nature. He had told her that she should consider herself extremely lucky not to be facing more serious consequences on this occasion. He hated the duplicity of his own words, but didn't know what else he could do, better she thought he had weighed all the known facts and was being lenient, taking into account her usual dedication and exemplary performance, than knowing Stephenson had little or no respect for her, her career or the tragic demise of the beleaguered Mrs Mazur.

It had been obvious that Claire had expected and prepared herself for the possibility of receiving a much greater penalty, but despite the actual outcome of the meeting there had been no celebration, no evidence of relief; instead their encounter remained extremely intense, a sombre Claire only confirming that she was sorry for the mistake, for letting him down and providing reassurances that it wouldn't happen again.

******

He pulled up behind Ishan's car outside of the McKenzie home and inhaled slowly and deeply. He watched as Ishan was climbing out of his car and knowing he had no choice in the matter he moved to join him on the pavement. Ishan was scrutinising the ground as they fortified themselves ahead of the meeting with the family; informing a family that they had no answers and that none were expected to be forthcoming in the foreseeable future was high up amongst the scenarios every officer dreaded. Officially the case would remain open and active, but with the officers being reassigned

Justice

to other cases, unless fresh evidence was to miraculously materialise, they knew only too well that realistically, in terms of resolving any of the questions for the family, the case was in effect already as cold as ice.

The meeting was as they had expected. Mrs McKenzie was as dignified and stoic as they had come to expect, an air of calm surrounding the few questions she had asked, which were mainly around police procedures when a case was classed as cold. In direct contrast Mr McKenzie had said very little beyond a cursory greeting of good afternoon. They had become accustomed to his silences, he was the very definition of broken and as Tommy studied him he questioned if he was even able to comprehend what was being said anymore. In different circumstances he may have regarded him as weak, even pathetic, but given that his life had collapsed around him Tommy pitied the husk of a man sat before him. He recognised the overwhelming sadness of losing someone you truly love, he had felt that excruciating pain himself, and he felt consumed with sympathy and empathy for John McKenzie as he mutely stared off into the middle distance. Annabel's sister Kirsty had been angered by their visit, the information they shared and it seemed their very existence, she had not stayed long and the reverberations from the slamming door as she made her exit, muttering how useless they were, seemed to shake the very foundations of the house, the sound of her stomping on the staircase almost drowned out the word, "incompetent" but not completely. In reality neither policeman needed her particular condemnation to make them feel any more wretched. Sandy McKenzie had quickly apologised for her daughter's behaviour and both men had managed a half smile as they made to leave.

At the door Sandy extended a hand and simply thanked them for everything they had done. Somehow this final polite act seemed to hurt Tommy greatly.

Justice

On the pavement Tommy gave a quick cough before lifting his head and announcing "I'm off then, see you tomorrow."

"Yeah, see you tomorrow, Tom." a seemingly distracted Ishan said.

"Get yourself home, get some rest; things always look better in the morning fella." Tommy gave a brief smile towards his troubled looking colleague.

"Yeah, I will try. Just got something I need to do before I head off home." Ishan replied.

<u>Chapter 32</u>

Ishan had been sat in the car for over an hour, continually questioning the logic of his actions. He'd little recollection of his journey and as he silently watched what was developing into a glorious sunset the raging internal argument was finally coming to a close. "Stupid" he mumbled under his breath, what the hell had he been thinking? His hands gripped the steering wheel a little harder, he closed his eyes and buried his head into the cars headrest as he decided that he had acted totally inappropriately and was overstepping the mark. He knew this had the propensity to go terribly wrong and simultaneously considered the possible implications of what he was doing could have on his job. He took a deep cleansing breath and released it making an audible puffing sound as his lips vibrated. A sense of relief seemed to engulf him as he was suddenly very grateful he had come to his senses before it was too late, he would drive home, forget all about this crazy idea, try and forget about the whole thing, put it all

Justice

behind him. He opened his eyes and released his vice like grip on the wheel, but as he turned to retrieve his seatbelt there was an aggressive knocking on his window and a familiar voice asked "What the hell are you doing here?"

"I'm sorry." he stammered, unable to compose himself as he lowered the window "I understand how odd this may be for you and totally get it if you don't want to," he hesitated before continuing "but I thought…" What, what had he thought, he was struggling to remember and blurted out "… if we could talk? Maybe?"

After only a few seconds Ishan had heard a slightly quivering reply "Okay. But not here. There's a pub on the corner, I'll meet you there in ten minutes."

Now as he sat waiting he had no idea what he was going to say, it was more than twenty minutes since the interaction in the car and he was just considering leaving when the door eventually opened and Oliver Jones walked in.

He remained standing, his posture and tone harsh, bordering aggressive, as he addressed Ishan "So mister policeman, what do you want to talk about?" He clearly felt more confident now that they were in a more heavily populated location.

Ishan gave a quick smile and said "Would you like a drink?"

There was an uncomfortably long pause.

"Why the hell not." the pure vitriol in the air now was undeniable and Ishan again questioned his logic in having created this situation. "This should prove entertaining if nothing else. Bacardi and coke." Came the matter of fact reply, as the legs of the chair opposite Ishan let out a screech in protest against the highly polished stone flags.

Ishan nervously glanced at his watch whilst he stood at the bar, his imagination was now running riot through a number of scenarios and possible outcomes resulting from this meeting, none of them good, but as the cheery

Justice

barmaid, wearing what would be politely described as extremely heavily applied make-up, handed him his change he resolved to deal with the situation in which he found himself; and so as he placed the drinks on the table he simply asked "What would you like me to call you?"

"Oliver is fine, thanks!" came the rapid and curt response.

"Not Kelly? Are you sure?" Ishan asked, trying to sound understanding, supportive and above all non-judgemental, although he was a little perplexed on how he could possibly convey that given their previous encounters.

"Please. Just don't!" The request was dripping with bitterness and with the expectation of finality but then, with an obvious tinge of sadness "It is what it is" was added to the conversation.

"I'm so sorry about the way I treated you, it must have been so hard for you losing Annabel and the support she gave you. I didn't see you at the funeral."

It was apparent, not only by the words spoken, but the pain on his face and in particular in his deep, gentle eyes that the officer's apology was genuine and heartfelt and that, along with the mention of Annabel's funeral proved too much. The tears Oliver had been wishing away began to silently spill from his eyes, shimmering incongruously in the bright lights of the busy venue.

Over the next hour Ishan listened as his companion explained how much he had loved Annabel, valued her friendship and missed her terribly. The conversation was honest, open and understandably emotionally charged.

They were both silent for a moment before Ishan said with a reassuring smile.

Justice

"Everyone is entitled to live their life as they want to you know? You can live your life as you want and you can be whoever you want to be."

"Oh, really? Is that a fact?" Oliver scoffed "It's that easy is it?"

"I'm not saying it's easy, but-" Ishan's voice was drowned out mid-sentence as suddenly a cacophony of words, dripping with contempt seemed to quickly tumble out of the young man sat before him in no particular order.

"I have 'brought shame' on my mother, as she likes to remind me daily, no hourly," the sneering within the words spoken was unmistakable "I'm lucky to still have a roof over my head I am. Lucky to still have a family. No one will ever accept me, no one ever has," he suddenly stopped speaking abruptly and looked down at the table. His voice was almost inaudible as he whispered "only Annabel, and look what has happened to her."

"What happened to Annabel was not your fault, I don't know why she did what she did, and we will probably never know now." Ishan felt so sorry for the guilt ridden young man before him as he continued, gently explaining. "No one has the right to dictate how anyone else should live their life."

"Is that so?" A new flash of anger found Oliver staring at Ishan for a split second before looking away to the right, trying to compose himself. When he eventually returned Ishan's gaze, the clearly distraught youngster asked "What the hell is it you want, why are you here?"

Ishan simply stated "You have lost someone special, someone who supported you, your closest friend. I figured you could do with a friend to help you."

Oliver was obviously dubious of the officer sat before him. They looked meaningfully at one another for a moment before the chair legs once again scrapped harshly against the stone and Ishan, to his relief heard the words "So, do you want another drink or what?"

Justice

After spending almost a further hour together, they had gone their separate ways. Ishan felt better about himself after apologising for his behaviours and offering the hand of friendship, but he had been conscious of the need to tread lightly and as such he was uncertain as to when, if ever, he would speak to Oliver again; but either way he was pleased he had reached out, taken responsibility for his actions. There was just one more thing he needed to do before he could finally head home.

Chapter 33

Tommy had been dozing on and off on the lounge sofa since he'd arrived home. He knew he'd be more comfortable in bed and he knew he was being stupid, but the bed he had shared with Cathy was full of memories of them together, and what he would gain in the warmth of the duvet, he would lose in the mental torment and pain of the stark loneliness he felt whenever he pictured her in his arms in their marital bed.

He was still feeling drowsy, but as he opened his heavy eyes he realised he was hungry. He lay looking at the ceiling trying to recall when he had last eaten, apart from two chocolate covered digestives he'd had with a cup of tea when he had got home he couldn't remember when he had previously had anything to eat. He groaned as he shifted his bulk to sit at the edge of the settee and as he leaned forward to reach the Indian take-away menu from the substantial collection of

Justice

menus he was acquiring, he again chastised himself for the way he was living. There was no doubt in his mind that Cathy would be unimpressed with the way he was letting things slide and he recognised the need to try harder and do better. He tutted, shaking his head in disgust at himself. Whilst simultaneously allowing his finger to search the menu for something that would temporarily fill the numerous shortcomings of his existence.

He was assembling the necessary crockery and cutlery whilst trying to avoid looking at the piles of washing up that dominated the worktops surrounding the overflowing sink. He cursed to himself and vowed he would definitely get his act together tomorrow, if for no other reason than he was running short of usable space. By the time he heard the rapping on the door he was feeling ravenous as he hurried from the kitchen into the hall way, as he opened the door in mouth-watering anticipation he was surprised to find Ishan stood on the doorstep where he had expected a delivery driver.

"Ishan is everything okay?" he asked.

"Yeah, sorry Sir." he cleared his throat "Sorry to disturb you at home, I wanted a word if possible?"

Tommy stood to the side extending his arm gesturing that he should enter, as he said "Yes of course, please come in, I've just ordered an Indian if you're interested."

"That sounds great." Ishan said with a broad smile, suddenly conscious he too was running on empty. He started to follow Tommy towards the kitchen when they were stopped in their stride, needing to answer the door to the welcome sight of the spotty, ginger haired, delivery guy.

They had both tucked into the delicious offerings like they had never seen food before.

"This is great, just what I needed. Thanks Tommy" Ishan said as he was busy clearing his plate.

Justice

"No problem, I always order way too much and end up warming up the remains the following day, so you're doing me a big favour," he rested a hand on his bulging stomach as he continued with a slight laugh "the healthy living regime starts tomorrow."

Ishan smiled, now he was here he did not know what to say to Tommy or how to even begin to explain his visit with Oliver, but as always his friend made it easy for him. As he collected the crockery Tommy announced "Right then would you like a coffee or something stronger and we can sit in comfort whilst we discuss whatever brings you here so late in the evening".

Chapter 34

Tommy wasted no time at all once they were seated in two large and extremely comfortable armchairs, coffees in hand, "So what brings you here tonight Ishan?" he asked.

Tommy sat quietly as Ishan started to explain that he had been to see Oliver earlier in the evening, how they had had a drink together in a local pub. Tommy listened attentively but said nothing as Ishan described how he had reflected on how the interview had gone and how he had felt afterwards about his personal behaviour in hindsight.

Ishan was an experienced officer, who knew the rules and regulations better than most, probably better than he himself. Tommy observed him for a moment before asking "What did you hope to achieve by engaging with Oliver outside of your professional boundaries?"

Justice

"To be honest with you, I don't really know. I was angry at myself for the way we." he stopped dead and took a deep breath before correcting himself "The way I had treated him. Clearly he is a troubled young man, with little or no support and it bothered me, I suppose. I wanted to let him know that it could be different, that he could live his life as he wanted to, that's all really, I guess."

Tommy studied the younger man before him a moment longer before speaking. He looked tired, less polished than usual and when he had spoken he was clearly emotional. It was quiet for what seemed an age before Tommy eventually said "It must have been difficult for you, having had first-hand experience of similar things." The sentence seemed to hang in the air between them, neither man seemingly knowing what to say or do next.

It was Ishan who finally spoke, looking directly at Tommy as he said "What do you mean?"

S. J. McDonald

Tommy gently replied "Well, I don't know what you may have had to personally endure my friend, but I do I know Em isn't short for Emily or Emma or Emelia or anything similar for that matter, is it?"

Ishan's usually handsome features seemed devoid of any expression or emotion as he eventually, slowly uttered "How did you know?"

"Well, I wouldn't be much of a detective if I didn't know now would I?" Tommy said with a warm smile.

An oppressive, all-consuming silence surrounded Tommy now and he wondering if he had said the wrong thing, played this all wrong, when suddenly Ishan said "Emmett. Em is short for Emmett."

After a little while Ishan finally asked "So how long have you known?"

Tommy gave a quick smile and replied "Well, let me see, maybe not the first time we met, but really, yeah, I have always known."

Justice

"And it doesn't bother you?"

"No, not one bit. You're a great copper and a wonderful friend Ish. You will learn from what happened in those interviews and, if I know you, it won't happen again. But if you are going to be of any help to Oliver or anyone else for that matter, life has taught me you need to fully embrace who you are. Warts and all" he added as he again placed a hand on his expanding waistline with a rueful smile on his face.

"Do you think the others know?" He asked in reference to his colleagues.

"Yeah, I should think so; it's not something we sit around discussing, who is or isn't gay, if you know what I mean. But yeah, I reckon so."

"Oh"

"If it helps I fully understand why you would have tried to keep your home and work life separate. But thankfully things have changed in recent years... yeah there are still some philistines in the service. Our very own DCI for one! But thankfully the dinosaurs are few and far between these days, and eventually they will be extinct."

There was another quiet period before Ishan said "I'm not being funny Boss, but that kitchen is a bloody disgrace. I don't know how you can function with all that mess." He paused momentarily before adding "How's about I wash and you dry?"

"That sounds good to me matey."

Part 2.

Chapter 35

The water was rushing up to meet him once more and he was finding it hard to breathe again. He knew the panic was not helping but he also knew it was now beyond his control. He silently called out to his god and in a split second made a wealth of promises about a newer, cleaner way of living, showing a greater compassion to others and even attending church if he could just get through this, if he could just survive.

There was a slight reprieve and he took the opportunity to fill his lungs as best he could. 'How the hell had he allowed himself to be put into this position' Tommy thought for a split second, but there was little time for logical thought as the merciless water was once again consuming him, drowning out both sight and sound and for a second all hopes of salvation. His lungs were burning as he sought that elusive last breath before his head was fully immersed again. Suddenly the force of the water was too great, he felt himself losing grip, falling, tumbling over and over through the crashing waves and finally he was spewed from the sea like a Friday night kebab on a cold Saturday morning. He lay where he was for a moment, the coarse sand against his face, not needing or wanting to move, just taking stock of his very existence and being grateful he was on the hard, dependable ground.

He became aware that the waves were rhythmically lapping his lower body, creeping up his legs, when a familiar hand appeared, out stretched and welcoming. Tommy reached up and allowed his friend to assist him to a vertical position.

"Oh my god, I feel like I could actually die right here, right now." He gasped, as Ishan was unable to contain his laughter any longer.

Once warm and dry and nursing a cup of hot chocolate in the 'club house' which was little more than a glorified shed on the side of the water, Tommy studied his friend

Justice

as he busied himself cleaning and storing equipment at the far end of the room.

"Well, I think we can cross surfboarding off your list of potential hidden talents. Definitely a once only kind of activity me thinks." Emmett said with a broad smile and a twinkle in his eye.

"Do you think so?" Tommy replied sarcastically before taking a sip from the cup he was cradling. He had been sceptical when Em had advised he needed a 'hot chocolate with all the trimmings' but as he consumed the much needed warmth and the additional calories he had to agree it was indeed what he needed to help restore his equilibrium.

"I genuinely do not see how anyone does that for pleasure." he said "Putting the suit on, was workout enough for me. Not to mention the utter humiliation of wearing anything skin tight at my age." Tommy quickly added, with the pretence of seriousness, "I have no idea how you talk me into these bloody mad capped ideas, I could have died." With this the two erupted into laughter once more.

As Ishan made his way to their table, complete with its red and white checked, plastic table cloth and chairs screwed to the floor he absorbed the scene. "What's so funny then?" he asked as he squeezed into the seat next to Emmett.

"Nothing much, we were just agreeing that Surfing was not the 'new big thing' for Tommy. But the quest continues!" Em said with a finger in the air and a sense of excitement in his voice.

"Oh goody." came Tommy's response, dripping with fake cynicism, before all three shared another quick chuckle.

It had been a little over four months since Ishan had introduced Emmett to Tommy and it seemed to have flown by in the blink of an eye. The two having got on so well from their very first encounter; he had seamlessly slipped into their lives, filling an obvious gap

Justice

and although it had never really been discussed Tommy thought he served the purpose of an older and as he liked to imagine, much wiser father figure to this kind and welcoming couple.

As he sat watching the merciless waves crashing on the beach he contemplated Ishan and Emmett as they stood at the stainless steel counter ordering food. Both were utterly committed to the other and the pursuit of happiness. They supported each other in all aspects of life and as his grandmother would have said they were, 'a good fit'. Yes they were both young and handsome with the world at their feet, but it was more than that, despite the obvious cultural differences, they seemed to dovetail perfectly. Emmett, as a social worker, was a nurturing and calming influence on Ishan and they really did exude a feeling of unity and love.

He was suddenly acutely aware of how much he still missed Cathy. He didn't consciously think about her all the time now and outwardly, to the casual observer, it would appear that he was, 'getting on with his life', which was something he was frequently encouraged to do; in fact sometimes, to his utter amazement it seemed any interfering old busy body was willing to stick their nose into his most personal business in order to impart their unique perspective on his life. Just last week an old, bent women shopping in the local corner shop had asked him how he was before then imparting her particular pearls of wisdom as to how 'life goes on' adding 'what can you do?' He had left the shop without making a purchase or having the vaguest idea as to the identity of this genius in social commentary.

"This should cure all ills Tommy." Em said, returning him instantly to the present, as he cleared away the used cups and placed a heavily burdened brown plastic cafeteria tray on the table. "Steak and ale pie and chips, with extra gravy, just as you like it." He then popped a pot of tea in the centre of the table as Ishan was busy unloading their own plates. "Shall I be mother?" Em asked cheerily as he started to pour from the pot.

Justice

Now as he watched the pair driving away, whilst entering his gloomy home he had to admit that despite the actual surfboarding, his day out surfboarding had been both enjoyable and therapeutic. He knew it did him precisely no good whatsoever being cooped up in this house, on his own all the time, he also knew in his heart it was not what Cathy would have wanted. She was always so outgoing and full of life, like Em in a lot of her ways. She had an adventurous spirit and loved new experiences, although she would probably not have been so gullible as to have been sucked into attempting surfboarding. He smiled as he thought of her and then shaking his head he chuckled to himself, as he put the kettle on, what would she have thought of him flailing about in that skin tight wetsuit today?

Chapter 36

"Morning Boss" Claire greeted him as he entered the office. She was usually early and today was no different, but of late she had seemed much quieter than usual, almost subdued. It had become increasingly obvious that she and Tim were not suited to work together. Tommy had attributed this to the debacle surrounding the violent death of Mrs Mazur. He honestly believed that the mishandling of that entire situation had played a role in the poor woman's demise and that would, of course, naturally have taken its toll on Claire. But he couldn't seem to shake the nagging feeling that there was more to it than that. But as Tim was only with the team for a further eight weeks Tommy had decided to leave well alone, hoping that the old Claire would be back soon.

There had been an option of extending Tim's secondment to the team for up to two years, but Tommy had decided, irrespective of the work force

Justice

issues he faced, not to pursue that opportunity and as such he had already started casually mentioning, none too subtly as it happens, that the end was in sight for young Tim; he did this in the main by means of statements surrounding work allocations, such as 'will you be able to complete that before you leave do you think?' and 'as that's going to drag on I will ask someone else to pick it up Tim'.

It was obvious that Tim was none too impressed with the situation, that he had hoped to stay within the team once he had established himself, but despite his bounty of enthusiasm for the job, Tommy had to consider the effectiveness of the entire team as one unit and sad as it may be for Tim, Tommy believed that Tim's presence was now a hindrance to the cohesiveness of the team, an unnecessary distraction, and therefore an impediment to the achievement of their overarching goals.

"Morning Claire. Do anything nice over the weekend?"

"Nothing much to be honest." She seemed preoccupied as she carried on typing, her eyes fixed on the computer screen.

"Everything okay?" he gently probed.

"Yeah, just busy. Carl and I are off to see this latest mugging victim this morning and I really need to complete this mountain of paperwork ASAP in case I get called this week, but in fairness I think Zoe Meadows and Ivan Kisluck are likely to plead guilty before the case actually starts." she replied with little eye contact.

"It would be good if they did, save the extended family from having to hear all the details of what they actually did to the baby. Poor kid." as he spoke he revisited, in his mind's eye, the vivid images of pure savagery that were central to their case and the securing of a conviction, images that would stay with all involved, images that could never be unseen.

"Well if they do plead out it won't be to save the families feelings or the tax payers money I can tell you that, they

Justice

have literally no remorse. No, if these two low lives plead guilty it will be for one reason and one reason only, the potential of a reduction in bloody sentencing, as usual!" Claire's anger was clearly visible as she spoke.

Tommy had long maintained that the crimes where children were involved were the hardest to deal with; he knew only too well how bearing witness to unimaginable levels of violence and depravity against the most helpless and innocent changed you, how could it not? He wondered now if the changes in Claire, that had troubled him of late, were in some way associated with this case.

"Yip, you're not wrong there Claire." Tommy said as he walked towards his little office, which occupied a small corner of the much larger open plan space.

"Oh. I forgot to tell you. Julie has some kind of childcare issue and won't be in today, but she said she's available on the phone as usual. When she rang earlier she said she had left some messages on your desk Friday night that need looking at as soon as you're in."

"Fabulous, I can't wait." he said with a sardonic smile playing at the edge of his lips. "In that case, before I get stuck in, can I interest you in a brew?"

"That would be lovely, thanks boss."

"OK, I will just get my coat off and then I'll put the kettle on."

Ten minutes later, he was finishing his cup of tea whilst he studied the messages, which the ever flamboyant Julie had hand written onto a number of non-regulation, garishly bright coloured post-it notes, which she had then felt the need to stick to the screen of his computer. Despite Claire reiterating Julie's assertions that they needed his attention forthwith, there was nothing too out of the ordinary for the time of the month.

He studied the six separate notes, all written in purple ink, pondering how Julie's pen-ship was a perfect

Justice

reflection of the woman herself, curvy, bold and totally non-conformist.

The finance accounts for the month are now available.

Detective Chief Inspector Stephenson would like to see an action plan before the end of the week, with regards the finance accounts.

I have emailed you a new policy with regards social etiquette.

Detective Chief Inspector Stephenson would like to see an action plan before the end of the week, with regards the introduction of the new social guidelines.

Detective Inspector Simon Jarvis called and asked you ring him ASAP.

My David has had a spot of trouble at school and he's going to be home for a few days. I have some minutes to type and I am on the phone as usual. I can sort the rest of the week out with my Mum. See you tomorrow X

Not for the first time he thought that it was only a question of time before Julie's perpetually innocent and harshly misjudged son David ceased to be a problem within the education system and started being a bigger problem to society as a whole. He hated to think it of someone so young, but barring some significant intervention and soon! It looked like David was fated to be one of their regular customers in the near future.

As Tommy mentally ordered the tasks, it spoke volumes that contacting Simon Jarvis was rated below trying to juggle the financial pressures they faced each month and way below the latest social guidance, which, if experience was anything to go by would at least be good for a laugh if nothing else.

Tommy was stood at the communal photocopier, printing off the pertinent documents when Carl and Ishan arrived.

"Well, well, what do we have here? Didn't know you knew how to work that thing Tommy." Carl said by way of a greeting whilst flashing a broad smile.

Justice

"Yes, yes, very funny, very droll. Just so you know Julies not in today, but she's working from home, so available on the phone if needed."

"David?" Ishan asked.

"Yip" Tommy confirmed with raised eyebrows and a knowing look.

By nine thirty they were fully assembled and as usual each officer provided an update to the team with regards to their workloads and progress. As Tommy listened he was really hoping Claire would not be needed in court at any point this week. They were short staffed already and Tim would be gone soon, they desperately needed more bodies, but before he had even looked at the monthly finance report he knew how unlikely it was that his boss would share his view.

By eleven thirty he was on his third cup of tea and knee deep in social etiquette reforms. The near two hundred page policy was a glossy affair which pictured officers and public alike in an array of different situations, all interactions seemed to be overly jolly and in all honesty Tommy couldn't help dwelling on how much time, money and effort had been wasted on explaining the very basics of how people should behave and interact with one another in the interest of inclusivity. Surely this was just a matter of basic good manners, showing courtesy and respect towards everyone he mused.

After a while with little progress, he had decided to play the cards he had been dealt, he would ask the team for their take on the new policy, hopefully they could generate some useful suggestions about potential areas of improvement, which could be included in the action plan and he would ask Carl for his input with the finance report.

Tommy had found that Carl's educational background afforded him insights which others, including himself, may be lacking. He seemed to see past the obvious and Tommy had enjoyed working closely with him on a number of cases in recent times. Carl never ceased to amaze him; what had previously been taken for a

Justice

lackadaisical almost laissez faire approach to work, was in fact a confident and self-assured approach to self-management. Carl didn't feel the need to justify every action he had taken or explain each blind alley he may have wandered down in the course of his work, he focused only on results; and although he sometimes seemed aloof, as is a common trait with many exceptionally clever people, he was in fact a very compassionate and caring young man. Tommy recalled now how he had been taken aback when Father Mark, the elderly priest from the local church had informed Tommy that Carl had been the only mourner to pay his respects at the funeral of an elderly man, Howard Scholes, who had died of natural causes in his own home. According to the aged clergy, Carl had explained to him that Mr Scholes was a war veteran and being present at his funeral to recognise his service and pay his respects, was the least he could do. Although he had not mentioned this to Carl, or shared the information Father Mark had imparted with anyone else, it had nevertheless had a profound effect on Tommy, he fully acknowledged there had been extenuating circumstances around the time Carl joined the team, with Cathy being so ill, nonetheless he had vowed never to judge a book by its cover again.

"Bloody hell" he mumbled to no one as he looked up, taking into account the yellowing polystyrene tiles above him, he recognised his mind was all over the place today, he needed to focus, he quickly typed out an email to everyone about the new policy and was half way through typing a message to Carl about requiring his assistance with the month's financial statement when the phone rang.

"D.I. Marsden"

"Morning Sir" Julie said "I have Detective Inspector Simon Jarvis on the line."

After a few quick social pleasantries were exchanged he resigned himself to speaking with his counterpart as he

Justice

finally said "Well, you had better put him through Julie. Thanks."

"Hi Tommy it's Si here." Oh how he hated the fake accent and the saccharine sweet tone of the man, but above all else it was the 'call me Si, because I'm young and trendy, down with the kids attitude' that really irked Tommy.

"Morning Simon. What can I do for you today?"

"It's just routine really, nothing to worry about, but I thought I would ring myself as we haven't spoken in a while."

"Oh, I wasn't worried." Came Tommy's rather dry reply. He was very familiar with his colleagues approach to life, if he wanted something, no matter how routine or insignificant it may be, it was always required ASAP and if you didn't respond in what he considered to be a timely manner he would set about chasing the answer to his request. It was widely accepted that what Simon wanted, even to the detriment of all else, was all that mattered to Simon.

"Thing is we've been investigating a murder and it seems that your team may have crossed paths with either or both the victim or the perp."

Jesus Christ – 'the perp' Tommy thought. This bloke really did watch far too many American cop shows.

"Really? How so?" Tommy asked.

"A while back you had a suicide, young girl, well our vic is head teacher at the school she attended and the doer is his wife, who is the head of social studies at the same school. So we just wanted to know, if there was anything of note...you know, did your team speak with them, was there anything flagged about either of them at the time." Tommy could hear what he thought were papers being shuffled as he continued. "We're really just crossing the T's and dotting the I's, but if there was anything we would rather know before it gets to court of course"

Justice

Tommy instantly recalled the Annabel McKenzie case, the school girl who had hung herself, it had been almost six months since her death, but he still had a paper copy of the poor girls file in the bottom draw of his desk, on the off chance that they ever discovered any sort of lead to explain why she had killed herself, of course they hadn't and in all reality probably never would.

"No, there was nothing, we spoke to the head master, seemed genuinely shocked that one of the students, a young girl called Annabel McKenzie, had committed suicide. Obviously his focus was on ensuring we didn't have any others following suit. You know how the protocols work." Tommy pictured Edward Grant, the genteel headmaster as he spoke. "That's a real shame, I'm sorry to hear that, he was a nice bloke. Very helpful, as I recall." Tommy was quiet for a moment before continuing "As for his wife, we did most of our liaisons directly with him, you know how it is, I don't even know if we were aware his wife worked there too. But either way, we had no call to speak with her, as far as I'm aware." Tommy advised he would check, but reiterated he was confident the investigation had not required the involvement of any of the teachers on an individual basis.

"Good stuff, thanks Tommy. We don't want it coming out at a later date that she told the police she was abused or some other crap to try and claim self-defence or some kind of mitigation."

"And you're sure it was the wife?"

"Oh yeah, absolutely, nothing says disgruntled spouse like thirty seven separate knife wounds does it?" Simon said glibly.

"Jesus. That is over kill." Tommy said quietly.

"Sure is!" There was a slight pause before he cleared his throat and added "I'm really sorry me and Sandra didn't make it to Cathy's funeral. You know how it is…"

"Don't worry about it Simon, given the choice Cathy and I would have gone to the Maldives instead as well."

Justice

"Yeah, well..." The silence was short but excruciating "Anyway, thanks for that, see you later Tommy."

"Yeah. Bye Simon."

Deep down Tommy knew his self-serving counterpart meant no harm, he recognised him for what he was, a socially awkward, tactless, fool. It was little wonder he regularly heard rumours of unhappy staff and HR involvement within his team. Tommy considered now, with a slight smile, that with the likes of Simon Jarvis and Dickie, his own boss, in the service, maybe the new policy on social etiquette was not only desirable, but actually essential.

Chapter 37

The remainder of the week had been a particularly challenging one for Tommy and the team. Despite the amount of overwhelming evidence against them; Zoe Meadows and Ivan Kisluck had decided to have their day in court, pleading not guilty in the murder of their eight month old son, Jordan Meadows, whose injuries were so extensive that some of the jurors had been reduced to tears on hearing the pathologist testify. Claire had been out of the office a total of three days due to the case; which mercifully had returned guilty verdicts on both, along with the judge's comments that they should expect lengthy custodial sentences when they next faced him for formal sentencing.

Whilst Claire was unavailable, given their existing staffing issues, it really was an all hands on deck situation. This obviously meant Tommy had rolled up his sleeves and was again leading from the front. He didn't

Justice

mind, to be honest, being in the thick of things was what he lived for, but he was also conscious, as the leader of the team that he had targets to hit and deadlines to meet and as a result he had resigned himself to working through the night on Thursday in order to get the necessary reports complied for the ever inflexible Detective Chief Inspector. Of course he had considered explaining the staffing difficulties to his boss once more, appealing to his better nature and asking for an extension to the deadline, but in all honesty he had previously taken that approach, when Richard Stephenson had first been appointed and he was in no hurry to go down that particular path again. And so after an already demanding shift he entered his office at six o'clock to start again.

As he sat behind the desk with a heavy heart he tapped the keyboard and waited for the computer screen to come to life. He loved his job, of course he did, felt fortunate to be part of the service he was so proud of, but the job was changing, society was changing, he was aging. He couldn't remember when bureaucracy had become the 'be all and end all' and it was in quiet times like this, sat alone in his pokey little office, that he questioned if the public at large would prefer that their hard earned taxes were used to fund more bobbies on the beat, as opposed to more and more trees being slaughtered in the name of progressive policing.

The computer screen finally cast a light around the dimly lit office just as he heard the external door open and then the internal office door bang. He looked up and was surprised to see both Ishan and Carl walking towards him. The two like him, had had extremely demanding workloads for the majority of the week. But unlike himself, they seemed sprightly as they hovered now at the door.

"Evening." Carl said whilst taking a sideways look at Ishan. The pair had an almost impish look about them and Tommy couldn't help but wonder what was to come.

Justice

"Good evening Carl, Ishan. To what do I owe the pleasure this evening? I thought you'd be long gone by now." He said as he glanced at his watch.

The two looked at one another and then back at Tommy but it was Ishan who spoke first.

"Well, we know how busy things are and how precious Dickie is about admin, so I have been collecting staff views to assist in writing the action plan for the implementation of the social etiquette policy, and Carl asked Julie for the monthly budget statement and he's been working up some ideas." Tommy sat speechless as Ishan continued. "We have formulated basic outlines for each of the reports, based on stuff Julie has sent us previously and well, we know Dickie wants these tomorrow and well, we thought that the three of us could get them done quicker."

Tommy was dumbstruck for a moment, when Carl spoke up and broke the descending silence. "We thought that Ishan could work on his report and I could run some cost saving suggestions by you and then we could head down to the Bells."

Tommy was bowled over by the kindness of the two young men stood before him, but was hesitant as to if he should accept their generous offer, the reports were his responsibility not theirs and they had more than enough on their plates as it was, he was also mindful that, unlike him, they had loved ones waiting at home they would want to see. However, it was as if Carl had read his mind when he added "Both Ishan and I are ambitious and we need exposure to more strategic management situations." he said trying to play down the offer they were so generously making "Let's call this 'on the job staff development' shall we?" he said as he raised his fingers in air quotes, before adding with a twinkle in his large brown eyes "Who knows, If we play our cards right on this one boss it could tick off a ton of bureaucratic nonsense in one fowl swoop."

A series of feelings were baying for Tommy's attention as he sat silent for a few seconds before standing to

Justice

speak. "Right then, let's have at it, shall we?" Tommy said rubbing his hands together in a familiar fashion, a beaming smile on his tired face. "And Ish," he added "I have warned you before. If Stephenson ever catches you calling him Dickie, god help you son."

Ishan had worked at his own desk, whilst Tommy and Carl were squashed together in front of Carl's computer. There was no doubt about it both men had done their homework and it was not long before both documents were rhythmically flowing from the noisy office printer. "Right," Tommy announced, "I'm off to the gents. Ishan can you bind the reports please and pop them on my desk? I think it's time I got you two a well-earned drink."

The Three Bells pub was busier than usual as they entered at around nine, so they were forced to sit in a corner at the back of the room on low stools around a small round table.

"Jesus this will do my back no end of good." Tommy said sarcastically as he eased himself onto the stool, before raising his pint in salute to both Ishan and Carl simply adding "Thanks lads, I would have been there until gone midnight without your help." The statement in itself was true, but he knew it actually belied the simple fact that irrespective of the time he had given it, he, on his own, would not have been able to produce the quality and level of detail they had achieved together.

"No problem Tommy" said Ishan.

Carl echoed the sentiment, raising his pint, "We're happy to help Boss."

"My goodness, I've not seen it so busy in here for a long time." Tommy said to no one in particular, as he looked around the noisy room, when an elderly lady, in an off putting lime green scarf tied impossibly tight around her weathered looking neck leaned in towards him from the far left and informed him that Thursday night was quiz night. When she then enquired if Tommy would be playing he simply replied without hesitation and a

Justice

beaming smile "No love, it wouldn't be fair, I have the very best team."

Chapter 38

"Happy Monday everyone! You're listening to Manchester Radio, the number one radio station at the very heart of our local community, with me Cassie James and Melvin Ferrero. Coming up after the break we will be playing todays *'Grannies Biscuit Tin'* where one lucky caller has the chance of winning today's jackpot; a massive fifty thousand pounds or a packet of biscuits."

"Love me a chocolate hobnob Cassie."

"Yes you do Melvin, but I know what I would want, given a choice of the two." Both presenters give a slight fake laugh. Whilst Tommy rolled his eyes, silently questioning the logic of whoever had thought these two had chemistry? Although he frequently endured listening to the nauseatingly sweet pair it was purely for the regional news and weather, rather than the on-line charisma of the vanilla duo.

Justice

"So don't touch that dial, because it could be you playing 'Grannies Biscuit Tin' very shortly! But first here's Amy with the news and weather.

"Good morning, I'm Amy Richmond and this is the news at nine. Greater Manchester Police have announced they have charged a thirty seven year old woman with the murder of local school headmaster Edward Grant. Mr Grant was found dead at his home on the twenty second of August following what police had previously described as a brutal attack. I spoke with the Senior Investigating Officer involved with the case, Detective Inspector Simon Jarvis, earlier today who gave me the following statement."

Tommy turned the radio up just in time to hear Simon's voice.

"After a painstaking and thorough investigation I can confirm that earlier today an individual has been charged with the murder of Mr Edward Grant." There was a slight pause before he continued "Mr Grant, forty one, was subjected to a vicious assault, in his own home, on the evening of the twenty second of August, in which he sustained a number of injuries, resulting in his untimely death. A thirty seven year old woman, who had been assisting us with our enquiries throughout the weekend, has now been formally charged with murder and shall be appearing in court later today."

"Can you confirm that the person charged with the murder of Mr Grant is Penelope Grant, the wife of the victim?" Amy Richmond's question was delivered perfectly, it was clear and articulate; the young news reporters tone having just the right balance of reverence to the deceased and excitement at the breaking news. Tommy suspected that believing this to be her 'big break', she had probably tweaked the original recorded version several times to achieve the final result, which now despite being short, oozed confidence and professionalism way beyond the young woman's years.

Justice

"I am not prepared to say anything further at this time; an additional statement will be issued in due course. But I can confirm that following a systematic and meticulous investigation, Greater Manchester Police are not looking for anyone else in connection with this matter and due to the hard work, dedication and exemplary policing methods deployed throughout the investigation of this crime, local residents can once again sleep soundly in their beds tonight."

Tommy turned the radio down and looked at Claire, Ishan and Carl in turn, gently shaking his head as he said "Told you, what a pompous arse he really is."

"I've already heard it twice this morning." Carl said

"Yeah it's everywhere." Ishan added.

"God help us if he ends up on the national news, we won't hear the end of it!" scoffed Claire. "It's sad though isn't it? He was such a nice bloke." Of the assembled, Claire had had most dealings with the now deceased

Headmaster. "Did Jarvis give you any idea why his wife did it Sir?" she asked.

"No not really." it was quiet in the small office for a moment after Tommy had added "Why do any of them do it, love, jealousy, money, revenge, mental break, take your pick." as he spoke he demonstrated each point on his fingers.

"Good job we've got good old Jarvis on our side then isn't it Boss? What with all his 'exemplary policing methods'" Carl quipped lightening the mood in the unique way that only gallows humour can.

******

"Well, that's that then. They have charged her." A grave shadow had descended over his sallow face, his lips seemed to be devoid of all colour. "Alexa, stop!" he commanded, the broadcast stopped and the ensuing all-consuming silence seemed to take on its own life form, continually expanding and filling the room.

Justice

He had been glued to the local news reports morning, noon and night in recent days, and when he had first heard the simple statement issued between other news items on Saturday evening, he knew in his heart that events would start to unfold quickly.

He had been praying that the news reports would remain silent on the subject of Edward Grant, but in reality he had known this day would come. He had felt physically sick as he had heard the initial announcement on Saturday.

"Greater Manchester Police have tonight confirmed that a thirty seven year old woman is assisting them with their enquiries into the murder of Edward Grant. Mr Grant, forty one had been the Headmaster of St Edmunds Secondary School and was a much loved and respected member of the community. He was found dead in his home on the twenty second of August. Police have declined to elaborate further on the development at this time."

S. J. McDonald

The brief statement, which had been shoehorned into a routine hourly news segment, was somewhat bland and yet he knew from the moment he had heard the relatively innocuous words his life and the lives of those around him would never be the same again. Initially, on learning of the arrest, he'd been consumed by panic, but over the last couple of days he had somehow come to terms with what would happen next, reluctantly accepting there was no real alternative; after all, actions have consequences.

As he sat now at the breakfast table in the deafening, unnatural silence he had managed a weak smile and simply said "Well, I had better eat something I suppose, it's going to be a long day." He reached over and picked up a slice of toast, as he buttered it he was already feeling nauseous, but knew he had to eat something. He knew what needed to happen next, he had played this day over in his mind many, many times, but that wouldn't make it any easier now the dreaded day had finally arrived.

Chapter 39

It had been an uneventful, run of the mill sort of Monday with the team working on a number of cases, at various stages. The daily team brief was straight forward and there had been nothing out of the ordinary. Tommy had decided to use the relative calm this unusual respite offered to review the reports he had submitted to the Chief the previous Friday morning; ensuring he was fully up to speed, ahead of their next regular meeting. He had no doubt whatsoever that the ever disagreeable Stephenson would have made up his mind already as to any course of action, however, he liked to be prepared, to put forward a reasoned and well balanced argument, but nevertheless he was under no illusion, the outcome of the weekly meetings were decided long before he attended.

As he looked at the finance report he was once again impressed by Carl's suggested solutions, in particular he was taken with the idea of asking Dickie to consider seconding three talented PC's to the team in replacement of Tim. Taking three junior staff would mean that Ishan, Carl and Claire would all be required to directly supervise a team member. Having three inexperienced staff would increase the workload of the team and of course carried inherent risks, Tommy was reminded of a previous domestic violence case which Claire and Tim had unfortunately mishandled with dire consequences, but on the other hand Tommy was confident that Claire had learned from the tragic death of Mrs Mazur and there had been no other performance issues to concern him.

He thought through the pros and cons of the proposal once more and he had to admit that with some additional care with the staffing rotas, by taking three junior staff he could save six months' worth of the salary from the Sergeant vacancy they seemed to be continually carrying, without the added expense of additional overtime to provide cover for the gap. This

Justice

should be enough to balance the books and appease his boss.

He was just getting up to get a brew when Julie appeared in the doorway and informed him that the officer on desk duty had called, advising there was a gentleman in reception asking for him.

His cuppa would need to wait as he made his way down stairs towards the front entrance without delay. It was fairly uncommon to be asked for by name in this way; people involved in on-going cases usually arrived by appointment, if they needed to attend the station at all and so there was no time to lose, as this type of unexpected request to see him was usually an indication that one of his regular informants had decided to impart some information. Contrary to popular belief this was never done out of some revived sense of civic responsibility and a sudden burning desire to do the right thing, moreover it was because of some internal fighting between the local fraternity of lowlifes or a desperate need to get in with the authorities first when things had started to go awry, irrespective of what viewers frequently saw on their television screens, it was an extremely rare situation whereby informants received payment for information, moreover it was usually a quid pro quo type of situation. Tommy knew from experience that the information provided by local informants could prove extremely valuable to the police. He had personally credited his own local snitches with having provided essential information leading to numerous arrests and convictions throughout his career. To this end he had spent years developing his contacts, fostering relationships with some of the most unsavoury individuals, who he trusted to provide him with accurate and reliable information on a semi regular basis. With this in mind he could feel his heart quickening in anticipation of where this encounter could possibly lead. As he had rounded the corner, leading to the open reception he had a definite bounce in his step, suddenly the day was alive with possibilities,

Justice

his mind buzzing with the expectation of seeing one of several familiar faces.

On his arrival he tried hard not to look too deflated as he realised who it was waiting for him in the foyer.

Chapter 40

It was almost two thirty when Simon Jarvis had been summoned to the Detective Chief Inspectors Office. Personally he wasn't a fan of Richard Stephenson but he had had a good result, with loads of positive press, so he was feeling buoyant as he made his way to the top floor of the building. He didn't really care for Stephenson's management style, he liked everyone to know he was the boss and part of that was his interference in procedures and seemingly endless demands for operational updates, Simon smiled, no doubt he would refer to himself as being 'hands on' but in reality Simon knew he just wanted to bask in the glory of others, stealing the limelight. Stephenson loved a good news story and in particular the media attention he could carve out for himself. But hey-ho, if he had to share his success on this occasion that was fine by him, just as long as the credit was justly awarded at the next opportunity for promotion. "Oh yes", he murmured to himself, as he tackled the stairs in a cheery, optimistic

Justice

mood, he would share today's achievement with his fame hungry superior whilst ensuring he got what he needed from the situation going forward.

He rounded the top staircase, not even slightly out of breath and silently congratulated himself on his current physique; yeah his latest fitness regime was definitely yielding positive results. He admired himself in the full length window on at the top of the stairs as he took a sharp right, entering the management floor, and he had to admit, he liked what he saw. Maybe he should consider upping his personal training with the voluptuous Veronica from two to three days a week going forward.

As he entered the inner sanctum of offices, the ever present po-faced Margery had simply ushered him straight in, this was a good sign, as she nearly always made him wait outside with her for ages, he hated that, as she never really spoke and to be honest, he always thought if she did, she would probably have had nothing to say that would be of interest to him anyway. He viewed her only as a gate keeper of sorts, similar to a Doctor's receptionist. But he had bypassed her today. It was all going his way; he could almost taste his next promotion.

Once inside the office he instantly became a little unnerved. As expected Stephenson sat behind the wide expanse of highly polished wood, but equally unexpectedly DI Marsden was filling one of the two lower chairs strategically placed opposite their boss.

Simon who was not welcomed in any way or offered a seat was becoming increasingly troubled, as a surly Stephenson wasted no time before barking at him "What do we have on the wife?"

"Sir? What? Err"

"I said what do we have on the wife?"

Simon couldn't quite understand what was happening, he took a slight glance towards Tommy, who sat

Justice

pokerfaced, as their superior was becoming more and more agitated.

"My God man, don't make me ask again. What do we have on the wife?" each word was delivered slowly and purposefully as the colour was stretching up from the collar of his gleaming white shirt and was starting to glow in his cheeks.

"Well, let me see, on the night of the murder she was alone in the house with the victim. Initially she claimed the marriage was good and there were no marital issues, however, when we later confronted her with evidence that neighbours had heard them arguing loudly on the night of the murder and we explained that we had witnesses prepared to testify that this was a regular thing she admitted there were some difficulties in the relationship." Simon was speaking quickly and his discomfort was very evident, Tommy felt sorry for his beleaguered colleague as he stood, confused looking, whilst explaining himself. "She then lied about her whereabouts, claiming that following an argument, about money, she had gone out and drove around waiting for things to calm down, before going home and finding her husband dead. On finding him she says she called an ambulance and started to attempt resuscitation." Simon suddenly looked more confident in his assertions as he continued "When we checked CCTV in the area she claimed to have driven, there was no evidence she had driven that way or parked up in the area she described. She eventually confessed she had been to see another teacher from the school, in his home, the two, it transpires, having been involved in a long running affair." Jarvis took a breath before adding, "Oh and the blood splatter on her clothing was consistent with a frenzied assault with a bladed implement."

"You don't have the knife? She's continuing to protest her innocence isn't she?" Stephenson asked; his tone was calmer now as he addressed Simon.

Simon was unsure what to answer first as this eyes darted around the room "Yes, she's still denying she was

Justice

involved in the murder, but we have a solid case." His eyes locked with Stephenson's as he continued, "Obviously I would have wanted the knife, we have conducted an extensive search but we haven't been able to find it at this time. The working assumption is that she did the deed, covering herself in blood in the process, took the knife with her when she went to visit her lover and somehow, with or without his knowledge, disposed of it, came back and 'discovered' the body and attempted resuscitation in order to deliberately contaminate the crime scene and explain the bloody clothes. I have a couple of officers leaning on him still. I'm confident we will recover it in due time."

Listening intently, Tommy had to agree from what he had heard it did sound likely that Penelope Grant was responsible for the death of her husband. And of course it was true that in most cases you didn't have everything you would have liked nailed down before charging someone. The wife definitely seemed to have the 'trifecta' logically applied to all cases, means, motive and opportunity.

Suddenly Stephenson looked at Tommy, dragging him from his thoughts, and with a nod towards his colleague simply demanded "Tell him."

"I'm sorry Simon, but the wife didn't do it. I have someone in the holding cells right now saying they - ." Tommy started to explain but was cut short by Jarvis.

"That's ridiculous. That's what all this is about?" he scoffed dismissively, his arms outspread, indicating not only the office but the meeting. "How many times do cranks come forward claiming to have done something heinous when in reality they were at home, tucked up in bed drinking their cocoa at the time? Especially when it's a high profile case like this and the media are involved. Come on Tommy!" he sneered.

"I'm sorry Simon; it's not some kind of eccentric, trying to get a buzz out of an association with some random atrocity."

Justice

Simon was flummoxed, the colour seemed to drain instantly from his face, there was no sign of his usual hubris, as he stood silently and then in a small voice, whilst holding Tommy's gaze he eventually asked the most relevant question "Why are you so sure?"

"Because along with a confession, I also have the knife."

Simon looked like he was going to be sick, Tommy felt incredibly sorry for his colleague now as he said quietly "But I've charged the wife. She's due in court for a remand hearing later today."

"Don't we bloody well know it? My god it's a bloody shambles, an absolute bloody shambles". Once more Stephenson could barely contain his anger; Tommy had noted a quiver in his unnaturally higher than usual voice. He physically turned now, Tommy in his sight "Marsden as discussed, get me those bloody prints as soon as possible."

"Yes sir, I have already had a word and the fingerprints are top priority, I expect a result first thing in the morning at the very latest, but in all honesty I'm certain we will have a match."

"Well, let's bloody hope so, we can't afford any more cock-ups." He focused his attention once again on the pathetic looking man who stood before him. "Jarvis, you do know that until we get a fingerprint match to the assumed murder weapon you will need to continue the process with the wife, don't you? We can't release her until we have concrete evidence against someone else that negates all the circumstantial we have against her."

Stephenson rubbed his forehead before saying "That will be all Marsden. Let me know as soon as you get the prints."

"Yes Sir."

As Tommy exited the office he was shocked at the turn of events. He could hear Dickie's voice reaching fever pitch as he closed the door and just about made out the phrase "PR bloody nightmare!" as hostilities resumed.

Justice

Tommy made his way back down the stairs to the office, where forty five minutes earlier he had a left a gob smacked Ishan sat at his desk. He knew that by now Ishan would have collected the others together in order to hear first-hand of the events of the day. He also knew that for some, there would be a burning desire to know exactly what had happened in Stephenson's office this afternoon too.

Chapter 41

Tommy took another mouthful of his long awaited tea as he stood to address the fuller than usual office at just gone four o'clock. The noisy room was dramatically silenced in anticipation as he cleared his throat.

"Right then, undoubtedly some of you will have already heard some of this, but in the interest of making sure everyone is fully up to speed and to prevent any wild rumours getting out of hand, I will recap on all the events of the day thus far." He announced as he took in each of the faces surrounding him; he knew there would have been quite a bit of chatter amongst the officers already, unfortunately it was only human nature and so he found it always paid to clarify what was happening before gossip mongers were allowed to run amuck. He knew only too well that rumour, conjecture and misunderstandings could have potentially negative consequences for any case and conviction. "Around

Justice

lunchtime today Julie was contacted by the Duty Sergeant on the main desk." At the mere mention of her name Julie smiled smugly as she looked around the room at everyone present. The air of arrogance she radiated was almost palpable and a passive observer could have been fooled into thinking she had just single-handedly brought a serial killer to justice, as opposed to having just delivered a message. But Tommy let it go; Julie's inflated sense of self-importance didn't even feature on his list of priorities at the moment.

"As requested I immediately attended the reception and was surprised to see that Mr and Mrs McKenzie were present and had asked to speak with me." The room was deathly silent as he continued "Some of you will recall; they are the parents of Annabel McKenzie, the fourteen year old school girl who was found hanged at the beginning of the year." Tommy took another sip of the now cool tea before resuming. "Mrs McKenzie, supported by her husband, had attended the station in order to confess to the murder of Edward Grant."

There were a number of audible gasps of disbelief before Tim asked "She's confessed to killing the Headmaster of her daughter's school?" quickly adding, "Don't we have someone for that?"

"Yes Tim, she's confessed to the Grant murder. As you say he was the headmaster at St Edmunds, the school which Annabel attended, she's currently in the holding cells. And as you also correctly point out, yes we do indeed already have someone for that crime." He cleared his throat and took a breath before adding. "In case any of you have managed to avoid the extensive media interest surrounding this case, Mr Grant's wife, Penelope Grant, was charged with his murder earlier today, she too is currently sat in the holding cells." He tried hard to ensure he held an impartial tone, devoid of any potential sarcasm.

Tim whistled through his teeth as he then asked "Do you think she did it Sir?"

Justice

Tommy did not want to be drawn into the realms of speculation, he knew it to be a dangerous place in which to wander and constantly reminded others that they should stick to only what they knew as fact, and he resolved do the same here. "Well she says she did, but that's as yet to be proven either way."

Tim would not be dissuaded and to Tommy's increasing annoyance spoke up once more to ask "Why would she do it?" without pause he continued, offering his own suppositions "If Grants murder is connected to Annabel's death, he could be the one who had been sleeping with the girl."

Tommy gave Tim a quick stare, his eyes conveying intense displeasure. "At the moment all we know is that she claims to have killed Grant. As to the whys and wherefores we are currently in the dark. But as far as I'm aware D.I. Jarvis's team found nothing of interest in Grant's background."

"Is it true Sir that she had the murder weapon with her?" Claire asked.

"Mrs McKenzie did have a knife in her possession and that's been sent for forensics. Obviously we will know more once we have those results. But at the moment we are trying to establish if it was the knife involved in the murder" Tommy explained.

"Is it possible Sir, that both women are involved in the murder in some way, in either performing the murder or perhaps causing a smoke screen aimed at creating reasonable doubt to avoid a successful prosecution of either of them? Do we know if the women are associates?" Ishan questioned.

"Of course it's possible, anything is possible," he mused, "and that's why we need to work fast to try and get to the answers as quickly as possible, before we need to release Mrs Grant."

Tommy felt a burning desire to draw this impromptu meeting to a close, hopefully putting an end to any

Justice

further conjecture. "To be honest, given the fact that Mrs Grant was charged with her husband's murder earlier today, understandably, Detective Chief Inspector Stephenson had to be made aware of the fact that someone else had presented themselves and confessed to the same crime as soon as was practicable. As you would assume that briefing was quite a lengthy process in itself, which has unfortunately impacted on the amount of time that we have actually spent questioning Mrs McKenzie as yet." He was mindful that some of the assembled would be as interested in the details of what had transpired in Stephenson's office this afternoon as much as, if not more, than the details of the case. With this in mind he decided to change the focus to what needed to happen next. "Ishan and I will be interviewing her further throughout this evening to try and establish exactly what has occurred here. In the meantime Carl, can you do some digging into the backgrounds of the two women we have downstairs? We know that Mrs Grant was a teacher at Annabel's school and that the

McKenzies were actively involved in their children's education, so they will know of each other that way; but outside of the usual parent, teacher exposure, was there some other connection, did they know each other, and if so how?"

"Will do." Carl replied.

"Claire, given the time lapse since we were last actively involved with the Annabel McKenzie case could you please review all the information we previously had, there may be some small detail, insignificant at the time, but given unfolding events may now have taken on greater meaning and importance. Could you please work with Nick Prentice on this? Fresh eyes would be good; it's always possible that we just missed something previously."

"Yes Sir" Claire looked around the room, quickly spotting Nick Prentice, who she knew only by sight and from the odd casual conversation during their time spent together in the small communal kitchen. At the

Justice

mention of his name Nick raised his head and supplied Claire with a slight, fleeting smile. She had never worked with him, but he had always seemed pleasant enough. She felt sorry for him as he looked a little anxious. He stood beside a bank of old grey, four draw metal filing cabinets, huddled close to a number of other staff who worked for D.I. Jarvis, who was notable, only, by his absence.

"So, are we taking over the murder investigation now?" Tim asked. Diplomacy had never been a strong point for Tim, but this was unacceptable; Tommy bristled for a second, alarmed by what appeared to be a little too much excitement in Tim's voice for his liking. This alone would be bad enough, after all a man had been killed. He hated it when people lost sight of what was important. But accompanied with this, was a sense that Tim had practically no thought or consideration for the feelings of his colleagues, who were in the main looking somewhat downcast. They had not engaged in the meeting thus far, choosing to study the carpet tiles as they stood together in a small group reminiscent of penguins. Tommy thought that they must have been concerned about how the unfolding events of the day would affect them personally, their team, their colleagues and of course Jarvis himself.

"As yet it's unclear as to how this may pan out, I assume Detective Chief Inspector Stephenson will be able to advise how we are to proceed once we know a bit more. But as of now nothing has really changed, both investigations are still active and proceeding until we have a clearer picture. However, it seems prudent to share what we know about each case openly in advance of the possibility of any necessary changes. So can you work with our colleagues Tim, understanding key information and decision points that led to the wife being charged with the murder please?"

"Yes Sir." Tim was openly disappointed, at the perceived slight of being side lined from the action.

Justice

Tommy was silent for a moment before he looked around the room. "Obviously, whatever the outcome, having two, as yet totally unconnected women in the same station, charged with the same crime could prove extremely embarrassing for the service should it become common knowledge, and as such; and I don't really expect to have to say this, but none of this is for discussion outside of these walls." The resulting murmurs seemed to confirm the desired understanding. "This is a delicate and potentially fast changing situation and time is of the essence...therefore I expect anyone required to work to make themselves available." Again the murmurs echoed around the office space.

He felt troubled and conflicted as he made his way to his office, irrespective of what he had said to the team, as he had previously informed Stephenson he wholeheartedly believed that the finger print analysis of the distinctive serrated edged knife, now in their possession, would conclusively confirm that it had been the murder weapon used in the execution of the savage murder of Edward Grant and that Sandy McKenzie had been the one to wield it. Should that be confirmed then the main question would of course be, 'why?' Why had such a caring, measured and respectable, middle aged woman engaged in such a despicable act?

Chapter 42

Ishan and Tommy could see the entire floor of the open plan office as they sat either side of the desk discussing their strategy for interviewing Sandy McKenzie.

"Not much point in trying a good cop, bad cop routine," Ishan had quipped "it's not like she's trying to get out of anything… and let's face it she already knows us." He flashed a quick smile.

"Yeah." Tommy had seemed increasingly distracted since the short staff meeting had ended.

"Come on then, what is it?" Ishan finally asked.

"I don't know Ish. Murder, and not just any murder, a violent, crazed like murder. It doesn't seem possible, does it? She was always so…" he struggled for the right word, couldn't find it and decided to use "controlled…You know, you've seen her." he said as he gave an almost imperceptible shake of his head.

Ishan knew exactly what he meant answering simply "Everyone has their breaking point Tommy, you know that. I reckon there's only one way we are going to know what she did and why she did it, and that's to ask her."

"Yip, I suppose you're right." he conceded.

Ishan continued, "She's in room four and ready to go."

"Okay, let's do it then." Tommy said as they gathered some paperwork and readied to leave.

As they walked through the office and down the stairs to the home of the interview rooms and the holding cells, Tommy was aware of the sheer amount of people they encountered. Most appeared to be busy but some were clearly just milling around, hoping to quench their thirst for salacious gossip about the now elusive D.I. Jarvis and what was going to happen to him. "My god Ish, the vultures are definitely circling tonight. What's wrong with people?"

Justice

"Some people are just like that Tom, they love a bit of scandal; love to watch the downfall of others from the comfort of their high horses. That's why reality T.V. is so popular." He gave a quick smile, flashing his perfectly straight white teeth with his last remark.

"You're probably right, but it's a dreadful indictment of society. That what it is! As you know I'm not one of Simon's greatest supporters, but bloody hell, he's hardly committed heresy has he?" he said as they gave a wide berth to a bright yellow cone announcing that the floor was wet, the pungent smell of fresh vomit and strong disinfectant rising up to meet them. "At worst he's made an error of judgement."

"Yeah I agree, I really do, but you know what he's like, it's not that hard to believe that there would be more than a few people revelling in the tittle-tattle of this particular cock up, secretly hoping he gets what they perceive is coming to him."

S. J. McDonald

Tommy shook his head in despair as he acknowledged his colleagues comments "I suppose you're right. But it still leaves a nasty taste in the mouth doesn't it?"

As they entered the stark, uninviting room Sandy McKenzie was sat bolt upright, hands casually resting on the table, her fingers loosely interlaced. She was dressed in a dark maroon coloured shift dress with a matching jacket; obviously no one had seen a need to depersonalise her by making her relinquish her own clothing in favour of a white paper jumpsuit, as was usual procedure. It made sense, Tommy thought, it wasn't like they were going to find anything incriminating on her clothes or person almost three weeks after the murder. Her hair was pulled back from her face in a tight chignon, her light makeup slightly illuminated under the harsh lights. She stood to greet them with a warm handshake and uncompromising eye contact and as Tommy took his seat, he thought she would not be out of place chairing a school governors meeting.

Justice

Following the necessary formal introductions of everyone present, Ishan took the lead and explained the procedures, during which time she had listened and confirmed her understanding only by a series of nods. Ishan had explained her rights to her once again, and once again she had declined to have a solicitor present, as she had when Tommy had first spoken to her earlier in the day.

With the formalities out of the way Tommy began the questioning. "Mrs McKenzie, Can you please tell us in your own words about the events leading up to and the actual murder of Mr Edward Grant on or around the twenty second of August."

"Yes of course" she replied confidently, adding "and please call me Sandy, everybody does." Tommy was instantly transported through time for a few seconds as he recalled she had used almost exactly the same words during one of their very first encounters.

S. J. McDonald

She appeared to be at ease in the no nonsense surroundings, as she started to pour out the details of the crime. She seemed unbelievably cold and unaffected by her words. She had fixed her eyes on a spot on the wall behind them, slightly above their heads, as she recalled the days leading up to the murder and the ferocious attack itself in a concise, succinct manner. The tone and level of her voice never altering as she described her murderous actions; she was completely devoid of all emotion.

After less than fifty minutes she had remained unfazed as Tommy explained to her that they were going to take a short break, during which time she would be escorted back to her cell.

"Well that was short and sweet wasn't it?" Ishan said sarcastically as they dodged the wet floor sign on their way back to the staircase.

"It's not just me then?" Tommy said a bemused look plastered on his face.

Justice

"No Boss, that was strange to say the least. There was absolutely no point in asking anything else anyway, she gave us everything and I mean everything. Never seen anything like it have you?"

"I can't say I have, no."

Chapter 43

"Do you realise Ish, that in all the time we have known her, this is the first cuppa Julie has ever made us?"

"She's in her element Sir. Loving the fact she's played such a vital role in the unfolding events." Ishan replied with a huge smile.

"Ah well, every cloud." Tommy said taking a refreshing mouthful.

"Look out Boss, here she comes again."

Julie tapped on the glass panel in Tommy's door whilst simultaneously opening it and announcing "Detective Chief Inspector Stephenson's P.A. called. Wanted to know if you had the finger prints back in the Edward Grant case?"

Tommy cursed under his breath before replying "Tell you what Julie, would you mind ringing Margery back

Justice

and telling her we will contact her when we have anything conclusive?"

"Yes of course, I will ring her back right away. Do you need me to do anything else for you Sir?" A beaming Julie asked.

"No, not at the moment. Thank you Julie." At that the larger than life Julie closed the door, undoubtedly intent on continuing to build up her importance with anyone available and willing to listen.

"Nicely played" Ishan sniggered.

"I do what I can." Tommy said with a quick smile before rubbing his hands together and announcing. "Now then, let's get the key players in, they haven't had long, but you never know."

It was a tight squeeze in the small office, but they needed to scale things back a bit if they wanted to make the necessary progress. Tommy was all for inclusiveness, but sometimes he found the old adage 'too many cooks spoil the broth' to be extremely apt.

"Okay." he started "Ishan and I, have now had the opportunity to conduct a short formal interview with Sandy McKenzie. She's been extremely forthcoming, providing us with lots of information about the murder." he looked at each of the officers assembled before continuing "However, given our Initial assessment of the suspect, we both agreed that it would be wise to get a psychiatric evaluation done and therefore it was necessary to end the interview quite quickly. She's been returned to the holding cells and placed on suicide watch until a comprehensive medical review has been undertaken." Tommy explained "She just doesn't seem right." Ishan silently nodded to affirm his agreement "As I see it we have one of three things going on here. Either she did this murder alone, as she claims, and finally being able to release herself of the burden of keeping it a secret is proving too much for her, both physically and mentally, resulting in this

Justice

emotional 'shut down' we're seeing. Or she is involved somehow with the victim's wife and they have acted in partnership, collaborating at some, if not all stages and now she's trying to distract our attention away from the wife with the old smoke and mirrors for some reason or another, possibly with the delusional aim of creating enough reasonable doubt to avoid a successful conviction of either of them. Or she has had some kind of mental break, whereby she has linked the trauma of Grants death with her own grief, somehow convincing herself that Grant was somehow involved in Annabel's death and from there she's concocted some fanciful account of the murder, falsifying evidence and inserting herself into the centre of events. Whatever is going on I'm concerned for her mental health and wellbeing, so I think it's prudent to get her seen before we continue."

Ishan quickly added "As it happens the delay in getting her assessed makes no difference to us whatsoever; as we haven't formally charged her with anything as yet, and currently she's here voluntarily, so the clocks not running down," he continued "and we don't intend making any decision around charging her until we have the fingerprints, just in case it's not the murder weapon and as Tommy says she could be making the whole thing up."

Tommy interjected "She is here of her own volition at the moment, however, if that changes and she does decide she wants to leave, at that stage we will probably need to charge her… prints or no prints. So we do need answers."

Tommy continued "I know you haven't had long but I just wanted to update you all, check if you've found anything of interest yet and most importantly review, as a smaller group, what we know so far. Nick obviously you haven't worked in this team before, but I'm sure D.I. Jarvis uses similar techniques to take stock of fast changing situations, so feel free to just jump in and say whatever you want at any time, there are no stupid suggestions, alright?"

Justice

"Yes Sir." Nick Prentice answered quietly; he looked even more self-conscious and awkward in the small space.

"Here goes. Not for discussion outside this room at this stage. So, Sandy McKenzie says she killed Edward Grant because he had molested her daughter Annabel. She has stated that it was his actions that drove Annabel to take her own life and that she killed him out of a sense of revenge and in order to protect others." The office was still, the air dense, most had expected something along these lines, had assumed it was a likely motive for the killing, given what little facts they had, but it was still hard to hear it. Tommy continued "She says she acted alone and denies knowing Mrs Grant in any capacity outside of a regular school teacher, parent relationship. Carl, have you found anything linking Sandy McKenzie with Penelope Grant that would contradict this claim?"

"Sorry Sir, only just getting going really, but there's nothing so far." Carl looked disappointed to be reporting such negative news. Tommy had realised in recent months that he was essentially a people pleaser; he usually shied away from disappointing and unproductive endeavours in favour of focusing only on delivering good news.

"Well, let's keep digging shall we? Thanks Carl." he adjusted his focus "Claire, Nick have you got anything as yet?"

"No, nothing Sir." Claire said.

"Okay, don't worry guys." he addressed the room "We can keep at it; hopefully we will have the forensic report soon; that should shed some light on things for us." he paused to look at each of them, before continuing "There's no doubt about it, this entire situation is extremely difficult, what with the wife already being charged and all, but I don't want you worrying about what may or may not happen as a result." He was conscious of Nick's presence and didn't want to add to his unease as he continued "We need to do what we always do, be thorough and let the evidence lead us

Justice

where we need to go, no jumping to conclusions that won't stand up to scrutiny later, okay? This is a big enough mess without us adding to it."

He was just about to conclude when Nick suddenly asked "So why did she wait?"

The group turned as one towards him as Tommy asked "What do you mean Nick?"

"Why did she wait so long after Annabel's death before killing him, if she just wanted revenge or if she thought he was a risk to other children and that's what she wanted to prevent?" he looked at the others before justifying his comments. "The previous records clearly state there was no suicide note, so if that was the case and Grant was a paedophile, which we can't corroborate, she must have known before Annabel's death, let's be honest, if there was no note it's not like her daughter could have told her after, is it?" Nick was clearly getting into his stride as he continued. "So if she knew he was a pervert before Annabel's death and she wanted to protect the school children in his care, including Annabel, why not come to the police with her suspicions and let us investigate?" he took a breath before adding "And if she knew what he was beforehand and then somehow suspected he had been involved in Annabel's death, why wait so long to take her revenge? It's not like she wanted to avoid detection is it? She's come here confessing. So why didn't she tell the police of her suspicions at the time or act sooner, assuming she would believe that he would remain a threat to others during any delays?"

Claire looked flabbergasted, he had had the opportunity to study the case files for little more than an hour and yet he was so articulate as he spoke, seemingly confident in his knowledge of the case, their case. She hoped his performance wouldn't cast a light on her own, as she surreptitiously scraped repeatedly at the cuticle of her thumb.

"Good point Nick. Well done." The officer looked pleased with himself and perhaps a little relieved too.

Justice

"Ishan let's ask her about the time lapse when we next speak with her." Tommy said, before turning his attention to Nick once more "I find it hard to believe Grant was a sexual predator but no one knew. Even now, not one person has come forward with as much as a suspicion of wrong doing; how aggressively was the victim's background looked into Nick?" he questioned.

"To be honest Sir, nothing of this nature came to light. But then again we were concentrating on finding his killer, not really trying to pin him as some kind of deviant...But as you know, these things usually come out in the course of enquiries, you would have expected something to have been said if he was a child molester, her school friends were all spoken to..."

"We should probably speak with Oliver, or Kelly, or whatever, you know who I mean." Nick said "We never came across this person and from the looks of things they were close. So if Annabel was going to confide in anyone, about Grant or her Mother I reckon it would be him, or her, you know what I mean"

"Yes. Of course." Tommy mused before asking if there was anything else anyone wished to add and mumbling a quick message aimed at some semblance of encouragement.

Chapter 44

The bustling office, packed with noisy, industrious bodies beavering away was in direct contrast to Tommy's little corner of the world. He and Ishan had discussed their next steps and were ready to continue with the questioning of Sandy McKenzie. However, both sat quietly at opposite sides of the desk clearly frustrated. Their attempts to speak with the suspect were being thwarted by the lack of a suitably qualified psychiatrist to give them the green light to proceed. And their intention to contact Oliver, who at best would only be able to provide background and context were being thwarted by the hour of the night.

Ishan, exhaled loudly for what seemed like the hundredth time, his thin, sculptured lips vibrating as he pushed his head back to glance at the ceiling once again.

"Do you think they built this office around this desk?"

S. J. McDonald

"What?"

"I'm just saying, this desk is so big and this room is so small, you know?"

"Bloody hell Ishan, has it seriously come to this?" Tommy looked at his watch "Almost midnight," he said "and we're still sat here like a couple of bloody garden gnomes minus the bloody fishing rods, discussing the size of the sodding desk" he placed great emphasis on the word still as he looked at Ishan.

The two were silent again until Ishan asked "So, what's your take on all this?"

Tommy appeared to be deliberating for an inordinate amount of time when he finally said "I'm torn to be honest Ish. It's all a bit incredulous isn't it? I mean, we have had a number of dealings with her and she just doesn't seem capable of such an egregious act. It's surreal. On the other hand why would she-" his sentence was interrupted by the shrill ringing of his land line "D.I. Marsden" he said before making a series of

Justice

affirming noises and ending the short conversation with a few words of thanks.

"Well if there was any doubt before, there isn't now!" He said as he turned towards his trusty colleague.

Chapter 45

After they had taken a moment to inwardly digest the information, Ishan stated the obvious "We'll need to tell Dickie then?"

"We most certainly will," Tommy replied "and I'm not looking forward to that one little bit, I can tell you that!"

The two stared, motionless for a long moment before Tommy eventually reached for the desk phone again and asked to be connected to his seemingly permanently miffed boss.

Ishan listened in as Tommy repeated the information he had just received from the lab tech, "The knife is conclusively the murder weapon, apparently there had been little or no attempt to clean it, so there was still quite a bit of the victim's blood present and the fingerprints are an exact match to Mrs McKenzie." Ishan could hear a series of muffled questions and a couple of not so stifled curses before the conversation was quickly

Justice

drawing to a close. "No Sir. No doubt whatsoever, she killed him. Aha. Aha. Err. Yes the formal report should be with us tomorrow. But given the circumstances they phoned ahead to let us know the findings. Yes Sir. Yes Sir. Yes Sir, I understand."

A red faced Tommy put the phone down and looked relieved to have ended the short conversation, as he said "I would not want to be Jarvis right now."

"Yeah, me neither."

Within a matter of seconds the phone on Tommy's desk rang again. Ishan answered and Dave from the custody suite advised that Sandy McKenzie had been examined by the duty doctor, who had given the all clear to continue. Ishan thanked him and asked she be taken to interview room four, confirming "We are on our way."

Chapter 46

As soon as the necessary formalities had taken place Tommy asked if she would tell them again what had happened on the days and weeks leading up to the murder of Edward Grant.

She was now dressed in a white, paper jumpsuit, which in no way diminished her, she still appeared calm and confident, and surprisingly there was something of elegance about her, even here in this desolate place.

She looked at each officer in turn, holding their gaze for a moment before addressing Tommy directly "Do we really need to do this Detective? Surely it's all just academic by now isn't it? Surely you must have the fingerprint analysis from the knife, conclusively confirming that I'm telling you the irrefutable truth, I killed him." She never flinched, never faltered; the statement was so dispassionate, it was as if she were merely reading required groceries from a weekly shopping list.

Justice

"Please, why don't you humour us once more?" Tommy asked with a fixed smile "For the completeness of our records." he added, whilst absent-mindedly fingering a paper file that sat on the table directly in front of him. In reality the days of hand written interview notes were long past, the room being fully equipped to record any encounter visually and audibly from a number of angles.

"I knew what he was, what he had done to Annabel, I was angry, bereft. I knew we would never get any kind of justice and so I decided to take matters into my own hands." she spoke quickly and concisely, there was no hesitation or sign of emotion in her voice.

"What role did your husband play in the murder of Mr Grant?"

"As I have previously stated, I acted alone. He wasn't involved in any way at all, you've met John Detective, he's a good man." she said with a small wry smile, her blink extended a split second longer than usual. "But not a strong man." For the first time since she had entered the building there was a hint of sadness in her demeanour before she regained her composure and continued "He knew nothing about it until a couple of weeks ago, when I explained what I'd done. I told him straight that I wouldn't allow anyone else to take the blame." She gave a quick humourless laugh as she added "Poor John, he's been continuously monitoring the news since the moment I told him. I'm worried about him; he really has been most terribly affected by all this."

She came across as merciless, devoid of any kind of sympathy for the dead man, no empathy for his loved ones or remorse for her actions. She appeared heartless and Tommy thought almost inhumane. He found himself speechless for a moment as he recalled how Mr McKenzie had appeared, when he had attended the station and asked to speak with him. He remembered now how the man had looked very old, his skin almost transparent, with a greyness usually reserved for the terminally sick. Tommy had pitied the man on a number

Justice

of occasions since their first meeting, but none greater than now as he considered how hard his life must have been with this evil shrew. He realised he had zoned out fleetingly and heard his colleagues familiar voice.

"Where did you get the knife?" Ishan asked

"I told you before; I picked it up at a car boot sale."

"Which one?" he pushed.

"Ambers Wood Lane. Does it really matter?" she openly sighed and pushed her shoulders back momentarily in what appeared to be an attempt to relieve some tension. Her level of callousness was unfathomable as she continued. "I obtained the knife, I went to his home, I waited in the access road at the back of the house until he was alone, I entered via the patio doors and I stabbed him. I told you all this when we last spoke." She sounded detached, almost bored as she recalled the events once more.

"How did you know where he lived?" Tommy asked

"I told you earlier, I followed him from the school one day. That's when I discovered there was access to the back garden from the overgrown pathway, where the dustbins are stored. From there I could clearly see into the kitchen at the rear of the house."

After repeating some of the earlier questions and receiving the same, almost robotic replies Tommy fingered the edge of the paper folder in front of him as he asked "Why did you wait so long after Annabel's death to take your revenge?"

"What do you mean?"

"Well you say he was a paedophile, but we can find no evidence of that. If you in fact believed that; had any evidence of it, why didn't you come to us, tell us about your suspicions? Give us the opportunity to investigate." she was quiet as he continued "When exactly did you first start to suspect Mr Grant was a danger to the children in his charge?" she still didn't speak, her eyes were lowered, her brow pinched. "Why

Justice

are you so certain that Mr Grant was somehow involved in and is responsible for your daughter's death? Why-" his questioning was cut short abruptly as Sandy McKenzie suddenly looked up and met his gaze.

"I'm sorry Detective but I'm quite tired now, as you would imagine it's been a very difficult few weeks and an exhausting day." There was the shortest of pauses as she stated "I came forward because I wanted to do the right thing; I couldn't stand the thought of an innocent person going to jail for a crime they hadn't committed. I have given you the murder weapon and provided you with a full confession. I really don't know what more you could possibly need from me and I have no intention of reliving the experience of that night over and over again whether it be for the benefit of your precious records, or to salve your morbid curiosity and voyeuristic pleasures." Her face was fixed, her eyes held a fiery determination as she added "And therefore I must advise you that I won't be answering any further questions." From that moment it was as if she was sat alone in the room, she said nothing and despite all attempts she didn't acknowledge or respond in any way to what was being said, it was as if she could no longer see or hear them.

After a number of fruitless attempts to engage with the suspect, Tommy and Ishan made their way back upstairs.

"Is it me or what" said Ishan, his frustration evident in his weary voice "I just can't seem to weigh her up, she came in of her own volition, she says to prevent a miscarriage of justice. She comes across all 'butter wouldn't melt in her mouth', all prim and proper, like she's always done, but in reality she's acting like she's running the show." He shook his head as he spoke "Doesn't want counsel, wants to assist and be fully cooperative, but as soon as she's had enough that's that, rain stops play! I used to think she was a really nice lady, felt sorry for her losing her daughter and everything. Seems we had her wrongly pegged from the start. She's some sort of megalomaniac... She's getting

Justice

off on this Sir. I don't care what the medics say, she's not right, to do what she's done, the horror she inflicted. You saw the crime scene photos, and yet she's acting like we are booking her for a speeding offence, that we're some sort of bloody inconvenience she can do without."

"I agree Ish it's all very strange… Although in fairness we always thought she was a tough cookie. But obviously we clearly didn't know the extent of what she capable of, she's just so incredibly… cold."

"Makes you wonder what went on behind closed doors, doesn't it?" Ishan paused briefly before sombrely adding. "No wonder the kid ended it."

Tommy looked at his colleague, he looked as physically drained, as he felt, it had been a very long shift, with as yet no end in sight, but the overwhelming feeling radiating from the younger man, was one of abject sadness.

"Yeah, I suppose it can't have been easy having someone like her as a mother." He agreed with a heavy heart.

Chapter 47

By seven thirty Tommy found himself back in Stephenson's office, having been summoned to give his superior an update on the case. It was a cold, brisk start to the day, but the early morning sunshine was streaming through the window hurting his tired eyes. He felt cold to the very core; he'd had no sleep and couldn't remember when he had last eaten anything, apart from a slice of lukewarm pizza that was up for grabs around two a.m.

He had straightened his tie as he made his way to the management floor, but it made only the slightest of dents in his overall dishevelled appearance. He was exhausted and was in no mood to put up with Stephenson's usual game playing and nonsense.

From the moment he entered the room he could feel pure aggression radiating from his boss, his levels of annoyance had clearly not improved overnight. Tommy had not been asked to sit and therefore stood, like a child pulled out of class for misbehaving, as he updated the Chief on the events that had occurred whilst he was in his nicely tucked up in bed!

"What about the CPS?" he barked

"I have spoken with them and they have approved Mrs McKenzie being charged on two conditions." Tommy explained. "Firstly we wait until we have the formal report back from forensics to ensure it verifies the verbal report."

"That makes sense; given the shit show in which we currently find ourselves, don't you think?" Tommy was slightly taken aback. It seemed that Stephenson was somehow holding him responsible for the series of unfortunate events "What's the other?" he demanded.

"Well obviously" Tommy shuffled his feet slightly "Mrs Grant needs to be released Sir."

"Yes of course." he mumbled to himself, adding something inaudible.

Justice

"Well sort that then." he eventually said in a dismissive manner, before adding, as if an oversight "Oh and Marsden you'll need to continue managing two teams for a bit, until I can get something arranged. That bloody idiot Jarvis won't be in work for a while." With that he put his head down and the meeting was essentially over. Tommy considered explaining that this was not his mess to sort, that he didn't have the time to manage two teams and all that entailed, but instead he decided that discretion was the better part of valour on this occasion and quietly made his way to the door.

Chapter 48

It had been three weeks since Mrs McKenzie had been charged with the murder of Edward Grant following the release of his widow, but even now Tommy felt a clawing sense of shame whenever he recalled his role in the sequence of embarrassing events. He had, of course, apologised unreservedly to an emotionally drained and extremely relieved Mrs Grant, whilst predictably, her lawyer threatened a litany of legal actions against all and sundry.

Sandy McKenzie had continued to say nothing more on the subject of her ghastly actions, although when he had formally charged her he noted she too looked relieved the process was over.

The case had initially attracted some media attention, this was largely localised and as with all these things mercifully the interest was relatively short lived. Headlines ranged from the predictable 'Angel of death' referencing her career as a nurse, to the purely

Justice

sensationalised 'Slasher Sandy' and the more creative 'Mac the Knife' a throwback to a different era. Social media had used phrases like 'Murder Mummy' hinting at the reasons that a respectable woman would turn killer, but despite the heavy innuendo that Grant had somehow deserved the savage and brutal death he received, even the legion of arm chair detectives stopped short at anything potentially libellous. He had always thought that people were like magpies to a certain extent, but where magpies sought out the shiny and new, the general public was attracted to horror and gore, and unfortunately there was always something more interesting, more shocking, more violent and inhumane to attract the masses. Usually he hated that this was the case, but on this particular occasion he was relieved when the spotlight had quickly moved away from this particular debacle. No doubt the frenzy would start again when she was eventually sentenced, but with her pleading guilty there would be no trial to speak of and therefore he hoped that any future interest would also be relatively fleeting.

Tommy sat alone as he considered his next course of action. He had seen practically nothing of Stephenson during the immediate aftermath of the Grant case. He had made it clear that all media enquiries were to be handled by Tommy and for three weeks running, Margery had contacted Julie to advise that due to 'unforeseen circumstances' their regular meeting would need to be 'pushed back'.

He was still managing two teams and there just weren't enough hours in the week. He was concerned that it was only a matter of time before mistakes occurred and he worried about the dire consequences that could result. On a personal level, recent events had made it abundantly clear that under the current regime a simple mistake could result in his suspension, perhaps even costing him his job and possibly his pension. There was absolutely no reason for him to assume that his seniors would be supportive of him or anyone else for that

Justice

matter. But he didn't really worry for himself; it was the possibility of a catastrophic event befalling some unsuspected member of the public that kept him awake of late. He looked again at the bright white envelope in his fingers as he pondered his future.

Catching a glimpse out of the corner of his eye of Ishan heading towards his office, he hurriedly returned the letter to its home in the top drawer of the desk, closing it just in time for Ishan to knock and enter the office.

"Quick one, do you want to have a look at the applications before shortlisting?"

"No, if you just work with Carl and Claire, get their opinions; I'm sure it will be fine." he replied.

"Does Dickie know you're going ahead with three secondments yet?" he asked a knowing look on his face.

Tommy smiled "I have made an executive decision my boy." he said in a mocking voice befitting an elderly statesman, before continuing "After all there has to be some upside to never seeing your boss."

"He's a star isn't he?"

"Isn't he just! When everything's going well I can't take a pee without him wanting all the intricate details. No Ish, he'll find out soon enough that we have implemented Carls finance proposals when he eventually comes out of hiding, by which time it will be too late." he gave a quick humourless laugh.

"Okay, on your head be it Tommy." he smiled

"Yeah, like everything else around here eh." Tommy chuckled to himself.

Ishan was half way through the door when he suddenly stopped and turned "You haven't forgotten about Saturday night have you?"

Tommy cringed inside, he really liked Ishan and had got on like a house on fire with Em from their very first meeting, but he wasn't big on dinner parties. He

Justice

detested meeting new people he invariably had less than nothing in common with, especially in confined spaces with no possible means of escape. He'd never been a fan of that kind of thing, but now, without Cathy at his side to make the necessary small talk he was actually dreading it.

"Oh no you don't!" Ishan said in response to his facial expression. "Em will kill me if you don't come. God forbid the seating arrangements are ruined, I will literally never hear the end of it!" he stated in mock horror "You had better be there Tommy, unless you want my blood on your hands!"

"Alright, just remind me on Friday, Okay?"

"Oh, I will. Believe me, the stakes are too high not to." Ishan said, laughing to himself as he closed the door and walked away.

Chapter 49

By the end of the week Tommy wanted nothing more than a hot shower and to slide beneath cold sheets on his bed. The workload was unmanageable, and was becoming increasingly more so with each passing day that Stephenson procrastinated.

He headed straight for the kitchen on his arrival home, hoping a strong coffee would assist him with the evening ahead. He considered not attending the planned soiree, but Ishan had reminded him about it a number of times and he had finally acquiesced so he couldn't go back on his word. As he stood waiting for the kettle to boil he took in his surroundings. He had a cleaner coming in three times a week now and although it would take her a while to bottom everything, he had to admit she was doing a great job, it was nice to not have to fight his way around the kitchen in search of a cup clean enough to use. It was early days with the matronly like Mrs Bennett and despite the fact that she

Justice

left him notes about which cleaning products she preferred along with thinly veiled criticisms about how he conducted himself, he really liked her no nonsense approach. He poured the hot water whilst picking up her latest note which quickly informed him that the window cleaner he used was 'substandard', likely to leave streaks on the glass, she would prefer he buy her favoured brand, a thick cream, which he considered would definitely require additional elbow grease, but what difference did it make to him, he wasn't going to be using it. Once again she had advised that he may feel more comfortable if he were able to allocate some time to clearing the paperwork that currently resided on the dining table, allowing him to sit and relax at the table for his meals. He knew it needed doing and in fairness he had been trying hard to keep the place a bit tidier between her visits. He was however more intrigued by the final item on the note. Mrs Bennett had suggested she could make him some food during future visits. Obviously they would need to come to some agreement on the purchase of ingredients and such and she made it clear it would be 'nothing fancy, casseroles, pies etc.' He smiled to himself, "oh yes!" he said out loud to no one, work may well be dreadful right now but things were definitely looking up at home he thought.

******

When he eventually arrived at the luxury home of Ishan and Emmett he was still a little unsure of himself, of course he had spruced himself up, selecting a smart suit, shirt and tie and he had even brought what the fella in the local off license described as 'a lovely little wine', but as he knocked on the door of the well-appointed third floor apartment he was apprehensive of what the evening would entail.

Within seconds he felt his uneasiness progress to full blown anxiety as Ishan opened the door wearing a fitted open necked polo shirt with a pair of dark blue designer jeans and trainers.

Justice

It had been less than twenty minutes since Ishan had announced his arrival, shouting over his shoulder in the general direction of the inner sanctum, as he stood motionless at the threshold, dreading the night even more as he suddenly realised he had dressed far too formally for the evenings events. Ishan had been delighted to see him and no sooner had he called out "Tommy's here!" than Emmett had appeared, dressed equally casually, the array of designer labels somehow complimented by the kitchen tea towel casually strewn over his right shoulder. He busied himself wiping his hands as he walked towards him to welcome and embrace him, pulling him into the beautifully decorated hallway. He'd been quickly introduced to a young instantly forgettable couple, Hannah and Ethan, or something similar. Now as he stood awkwardly admiring his stunning surroundings he looked at his watch willing it to be later than was actually possible.

"Home time yet?"

Tommy turned in the general direction of the silky smooth voice as he explained "No, I was just..."

"Oh, I know exactly what you were just doing." the striking red haired woman interrupted with a slight laugh. "You must be Tommy?"

"Well, I don't know if I must be, but I am." Tommy replied, immediately chastising himself, what he was doing, repeating a cheesy line he had once heard in some second rate movie.

"Josie. Emmett's mother." she announced holding out a pale perfectly manicured looking hand "I have heard so much about you." Her voice reminded him of warm honey on a summer's day, she was nothing short of enchanting.

"Nothing too bad I hope?" the obvious fakeness of his laugh, fooling no one.

She reassured him that she had only heard good things as he gently shook her hand, his eyes taking in her attractive smile. She was exquisitely dressed in a simple olive green; long sleeved dress, the contrasting colour of which had an enhancing and enriching effect on her copper coloured shoulder length curls. Tommy wasn't much use at meaningless conversation; he didn't know what else to say to the attractive woman in front of him. He looked around the room for some kind of inspiration, his eyes finding a large striking painting.

"Do you like it?" she asked "I saw you looking at it as soon as you arrived."

God this was painful, He knew nothing of art but knew what he hated and this monstrosity definitely ticked his boxes for garish, pretentious crap. "Err...it's nice enough I suppose, but I don't really know art you see. It's not really something I would buy." he studied the picture as he spoke "It would be completely out of place in my house, but it looks okay here... I suppose."

She nodded as he spoke and then there was silence between them once more. He looked at his watch again then down as he shuffled his feet. When he looked up again he saw the woman turning to walk away. He silently cursed his social ineptness once more as he watched the woman, who appeared to be at complete ease as she worked the room with lithe movement and broad smiles. He looked around the room, taking in those assembled and when his gaze returned to the woman in the green dress she appeared to be fully immersed in a friendly looking conversation with a flamboyantly dressed much younger woman.

"Dear God." he mumbled under his breath, almost audibly. This was going to be a hell of a long night.

Tommy's solitude was finally broken as Emmett appeared in front of him holding a tray of the most delicate canapés he had ever seen. Tommy took one and devoured it, looking longingly at the tray. He hadn't eaten anything in anticipation of a free meal and his stomach was currently alerting him to an internal grievance.

Justice

"You okay Tommy?"

"Yeah, fine thanks, just a bit curious as to-"

"What time we are eating, by any chance?"

"Is it that obvious?" Tommy asked sheepishly

"Kinda, yeah. Follow me to the kitchen and I'll get you something to keep you going."

"See, I knew there was a reason I liked you." Tommy said with a broad smile.

He had been perched on a tall stool at the breakfast bar overlooking the smooth running of the kitchen for around ten minutes when Emmett's mother appeared in the door way. She asked if there was anything she could help with and when it was confirmed that all was under control she turned her attention to Tommy.

"So this is where you are hiding is it?" she smiled as she spoke.

"I'm not so much hiding as supervising the proceedings." he reciprocated her confident smile "And someone has to test the food to ensure it's up to muster don't they?" he said indicting the now empty side plate in front of him.

"I see," she replied "and is everything to your satisfaction?" she asked with raised eyebrows.

"Oh yes. I'm quietly confident the boys have this sorted to the nth degree." he replied with a slight but genuine laugh.

There was a slight moment of silence between them, but this time it didn't feel awkward or forced when the conversation eventually continued. Josie talked easily about Ishan and Emmett and their life together, she asked about him, his job and his life and he was surprised to find he was relaxed in her company, he hadn't really felt comfortable in his own skin since Cathy's death. He was even more surprised to find that when they had been ushered into the dining room he

Justice

had been relieved that they were sat next to each other so that the conversation could continue to flow.

"So, what do you do Josie?" he asked between courses.

"Oh, I'm an artist." she replied, a knowing look on her face.

"No!" he said with genuine horror plastering his features.

"Oh yes." she giggled, indicating the direction of the painting he had commented on with a slight head movement "That's one of mine."

He was silent for a beat before concluding "There's no way back from that is there?" he asked laughingly.

"Not really. No" she replied seemingly sharing the humour of the situation.

They seemed to have so little in common but despite that, or maybe because of it, he was intrigued by what she had to say and as the night wore on he was enjoying her company so much he was glad, despite his initial reservations, he had attended.

As he sat in the back of the taxi heading home he reflected on his first real venture out in a long time. It had been a success overall. The food was delicious and the conversation was stimulating, he couldn't recall when he had last had such a good time, certainly not since Cathy had become ill and he couldn't recall ever meeting anyone quite like Josie.

He signed contentedly as he edged forward to ensure the driver didn't miss his turning.

Chapter 50

The weekend had gone by so quickly; he could hardly believe it was Monday again. As he lay in bed despising the alarm clock he took stock of his achievements over the last couple of days, silently congratulating himself on the numerous accomplishments. In recent months he had practically made an art form of procrastination, but in direct contrast, this weekend, he had been extremely productive, making a strong start on all the jobs he had been avoiding. On Saturday he had spent a much needed morning in the garden, pruning, weeding, and brushing the paths of fallen leaves, twigs and general debris. It looked better, but not great, he'd never been much of a gardener. He had also managed to squeeze in a visit to 'Arnold's Gentleman's Grooming Emporium' housed in a black and white building, whose exterior was as grand as it sounded, that had stood at the edge of the high street for as long as he could remember. The now decrepit barber, whose real name was Giuseppe, was still as sharp as the razors he used, and Tommy had never failed to be anything but completely happy with both his services and the chit chat in the opulent surroundings. He unconsciously ran a hand against the back of his head, acknowledging that his personal grooming had been lacking of late, he was pleased he had made the time for both a haircut and one of Giuseppe's luxurious hot towel and wet shave combos. On Sunday there had been a rare visit to Cathy's grave, he didn't feel the need to visit regularly but for some reason he had been compelled to call in and tidy the place up a bit, taking a small posy of brightly coloured flowers from the nearby florist that he was sure she would have liked; before getting stuck into the never ending supply of paperwork. As he reviewed the weekend he smiled contentedly as he recalled, without a doubt, his greatest achievement, which was to agree a menu of basic hearty meals and sort out payment arrangements with the formidable Mrs Bennett. He smiled as he recalled how he had also managed to find

Justice

the time to tidy the dining table, so that should please the finicky old battle axe when she arrived later today. His smile extended as he considered what she might feel the need to pull him up about next; given the table was now paperwork free.

Facing the reality that he could no longer delay the process he eventually climbed out of bed and headed for the bathroom, wondering as he did so, how he might find a reliable gardener.

******

Once at the office he remained good natured despite receiving an infinite amount of good humoured gibes and comments about his freshly cut hair, general appearance and overall demeanour.

Over the last few weeks he had been taking briefings and updates from his team at nine, then calling into the adjacent offices and repeating the process with the team usually managed by DI Jarvis.

S. J. McDonald

In order to support all the staff, oversee progress and provide advice and guidance as and when needed, he was in effect tethered to his office, something he had always had an intense disliking for, his personal mantra being that effective leaders needed to be out and about, leading from the front. But given the circumstances and lack of support from his peers or senior officers he didn't see any other way forward. It was a tall order but he was somehow managing to balance the demands on his time, although he had an almost constant nagging uneasiness that he was missing something important, due to a workload that was the very definition of excessive. As he sat in his office considering his current position there could be only one conclusion, this situation wasn't practicable, it could only ever be a short term solution, a sticking plaster, and it had already greatly exceeded any reasonable time frames.

By the early afternoon he had received updates from all the staff, advised in detail on a number of on-going investigations including a spate of muggings that, as yet,

Justice

may or may not be related, an unfortunate incident involving a lad on an electric scooter and the disappearance of a social media influencer, who he was reliably informed was in fact 'TikTok famous' and he had spoken to a particularly obnoxious buildings maintenance officer about a backed up toilet, that was creating a great deal of upset and inconvenience to female staff members and which, according to Julie, there had been no responses to the numerous requests previously made to have the pungent toilet addressed; and now he was fully engrossed reviewing staff cover for the following weekend, given he had gaps in the rotas from both long held vacancies and short term sickness. The whole situation felt like one massive game of jenga, one false move and everything could come crashing down around him.

Julie had just gone to make a cup of tea and he was grateful for the quiet her absence produced as he critically appraised the staffing rosters. He was so preoccupied that when his land line rang he absent-mindedly picked it up and announced himself.

"Good afternoon Detective, or may I call you Tommy." the soft voice was unmistakable.

"Josie?"

"Yes."

"What err…" his brain was scrambling, he had had a little to drink on Friday night, but he was sure he hadn't given her his number.

"I hope you don't mind but I asked Emmett for your number." she said as if reading his mind.

"Err…I-" he started to speak but was quickly interrupted.

"-it's just that I said I would show you around my gallery and…well we didn't make any concrete arrangements. So I thought…"

Justice

The line was deathly quiet until she spoke again, this time she sounded less confident and self-assured.

"...unless of course I have misunderstood."

The silence was deafening before she then added.

"I'm terribly sorry to have troubled you."

As she was moving the phone from her ear she finally heard him speak.

"No, I'm sorry; it's no trouble at all. You just kind of took me by surprise. I wasn't expecting you to call and I'm having a bit of a bad day."

"I'm really sorry to hear that." Tommy heard her say, and for some reason he believed her. "I've called at a bad time."

He took a deep breath steadying himself before saying "Please don't worry about it, there aren't actually any good times at the moment. I'm meeting myself coming back." then he surprised himself as he added. "But I'm glad you called, and I would like to see your work. Clearly I'm a bit of a Neanderthal where art is concerned." he gave a slight nervous laugh.

The next couple of minutes were a bit of a blur and as he put the phone down he was silent for a moment. What had just happened? He had agreed to meet with her tomorrow evening. Was this a…date…did he have an actual date, with a woman? No, surely not. He considered now; how once she had quickly provided an address and time; she had ended the call with a statement about how much she was looking forward to seeing him again.

"Here you go, brought you a couple of chocolate digestives too; your favourites." Julie said as she placed a try on the messy desk. "You Okay Tommy?" She asked as she took in the scene.

"Yeah, sure." came the unconvincing reply.

"Now let's get this staffing sorted shall we?" He picked up his drink and took a large warming gulp. "Join the

Justice

police service they said. It will be exciting they said." He said picking up a pencil strewn piece of A4 paper as he gave Julie a wry smile.

Chapter 51

After yet another ridiculously busy day he found himself at the address Josie had given him on the phone the day before. The imposing, double fronted building had two large, slightly bowed windows either side of the tiled entrance and was largely painted white, with an eye catching sign that clearly announced to the world, in sizable gold lettering, that this was "A splash of colour" directly below the gold lettering and in direct contrast it simply said "by Josie" in smaller more modern looking letters in an array of different colours. He hadn't known what to expect and as he stood in the half light of a drizzly Manchester evening he was surprised and impressed at the vibrant space.

There were a number of people inside and it took him a few minutes to spot Josie, who was holding court with a well-heeled, older couple towards the back of the room. Her hand gestures and unwavering eye contact

Justice

gave the impression of pure passion as she spoke and for a moment Tommy envied the sheer joy she seemed to be extracting from the painting she was engaging with.

As he made his way across the room he was offered something in a tall flute glass from a young woman in a long white apron which he quickly refused. He was wondering what to do next and trying to feign interest in the surroundings when Josie looked up and caught his eye gesturing that she would be a few minutes.

When she eventually joined him he was studying a small black and white affair that seemed to him to be some sort of utopian view of an old, turn of the century, factory.

"I really like this one." he said with a slight head tilt. "You're obviously talented."

"If only; that's not one of mine. In order to run a gallery like this it's essential to keep things fresh and exciting."

She explained that along with her own work she often showcased the work of budding young artists looking to make a break in the business, along with regularly showing the works of a handful of more establish artists.

Tommy studied her intently as she continued to talk.

"Open events like tonight's, ensure that the artists get the exposure they need and I get a percentage of anything sold, which keeps everything ticking over nicely." She smiled as she pointed out a series of coloured dots close to each picture which indicated which ones were sold.

"It looks like you are having a good night?"

"Oh yes, it's going very well. Are you Okay to hang on a bit, its largely done and I should be free shortly. Then I can show you around properly."

"Yeah, no problem. Sounds good." he mumbled as she was already walking away.

Justice

Tommy was enthralled as he watched her glide around the room seemingly enchanting almost everyone she spoke to.

When Josie was eventually seeing the last of the customers out of the door and the young women with the long apron had started to clear away the last of the discarded glasses. Josie gave him the personalised tour. She was eloquent as she spoke, conveying not just an in-depth knowledge, but also an almost childlike enthusiasm rarely seen in an adult. He didn't understand everything Josie said, nevertheless, her love of the subject was both obvious and contagious and Tommy was shocked when he finally looked at his watch.

"I need to be making tracks, work tomorrow and..." he said with a shrug as he hovered near the door.

"Well, I'm so glad you came, Tommy, I hope to see you again soon." she had said as she'd closed the door.

S. J. McDonald

As he walked through the damp streets towards his car, Tommy was also glad he had attended the gallery event.

Chapter 52

The next morning Tommy was in the office bright and early. When Ishan arrived they exchanged a cursory greeting before he had retreated to the kitchen to make them both a drink.

"How's it going Boss?" he asked as he sat down hard on the opposite side of the desk.

"Same old, same old I'm afraid."

"No sign of Stephenson yet?" he asked as he gingerly dunked a digestive biscuit into his tea.

Tommy's response was both non-verbal and abundantly clear.

"Still no word on Jarvis either?"

"Not a peep." he gave a slight shake of his head as he added "Honestly Ishan it's all dragging on just a bit too bloody long for my liking. It's an impossible situation."

Ishan was quiet for a beat, before articulating his concern for his old friend, "You look tired Tom."

"Yeah. I feel it too." he gave an audible sigh. "There are far too many plates in the air right now and I can't help feeling that I'm missing something all the time."

"You're bound to feel that way. It's nothing short of a monumental shit show. And Stephenson is an absolute joke. No one could expect – Bugger!" He stopped talking abruptly as one of the digestive biscuits he was devouring snapped off and splashed into his brightly painted mug.

"Yeah well." was the only distracted reply Tommy afforded him, as he watched Ishan doing battle with his tea stained white shirt.

Ishan was still fiddling with the damp spot, an obvious blight on his usual pristine appearance, when Julie knocked on the door whilst simultaneously filling the small office space with her presence.

Justice

"Morning Julie." they said in unison.

"Detective Chief Inspector Stephenson wants to see you," she blurted out followed by a rushed "oh yeah, good morning."

Tommy looked at Ishan as he asked Julie "When?"

"Well, now Sir." She looked flustered and anxious as she spoke.

"Why the hell wouldn't he?" he asked with a humourless smirk and a shake of his head "It's not like I have anything else to do, is it?" He said as his arms took in the desk and the general surroundings.

"I'm sorry Tommy, but I have his PA Margery on hold. She wants me to confirm your attendance."

Fingering his freshly coiffed mane of thick grey hair, he slipped his hands to the back of his head, feeling the contrasting stubble as he took a steadying breath before calmly opening his eyes and reassuring Julie that everything was alright, advising her he would be available in about thirty minutes. He then used that time to get Ishan up to speed on everything so that he could hold the fort.

He arrived on the management floor around forty-five minutes later and despite the fact he had been summoned, along with the fact that he was slightly later than agreed, he was not surprised to discover that he was expected to sit in the company of the ever dour personal assistant for no obvious reason.

When she eventually announced that he may go into his senior's office it took monumental resolve to prevent him commenting on the ridiculousness of it all.

******

"Ah, Marsden, this won't take long." Stephenson said before looking up. "I just wanted to let you know that Jarvis will be back on Monday. So if you could get him up to speed Monday morning, it's business as usual." he gave a slight cough before adding. "Right then. As you were."

Justice

Tommy remained unmoved for a beat, despite the clear dismissal, until his boss lifted his head and asked "Was there anything else Marsden?"

"Is that it?" He asked, an obvious anger accompanying a tone clearly verging on insubordination.

Stephenson seemed genuinely confused as he took in Tommy's demeanour.

"I can't think of anything else?"

"No! I bet you can't! That's the bloody problem isn't it? I don't suppose it's ever crossed your mind just -" The air was thick as Tommy was stopped in his tracks.

"-I suggest you stop right there detective, before you say something you may regret." The red faced Stephenson demanded.

"Something I may regret. Something I may regret. Jesus Christ man! We are way past that! Sir!" the title used was a noticeable slur.

As he turned and walked towards the door, Tommy simply called over his shoulder that the time for talking was done.

It was action that was called for now.

Chapter 53

It was a cold damp and dismal Friday afternoon as he looked out over the garden. It had been four days since Josie had called him, three days since he'd been to the art gallery and two days since he had left Stephenson's office. Stopping briefly in his own office just long enough to pick up his coat, retrieve the letter that had been sitting in the top draw of the desk for a number of weeks and to advise Ishan that he was going home.

On his way home he had stopped only once; that had been to drop the white crisp envelope into a post box at the edge of the large park close to his home. As he heard the envelope fall he took a moment to absorb the enormity of the simple action.

Now as he sat in his favourite armchair he mentally took stock of the week. He wasn't concerned about work or the team for that matter, they were in safe hands with Ishan and the current madness would end after

Monday. Once Simon was back in work things would start to calm down, he could relinquish all responsibilities for that team and concentrate on his own.

The last couple of days had dragged, but he fully recognised he needed to be out of the office at the moment, he needed a break, but it was more than work that troubled his weary mind.

Josie hadn't bothered to get in touch with him since the gallery visit and he reflected that maybe that was for the best; after all he'd made no attempt to contact her either. What had he been thinking? He dismissed the intruding thoughts and tried to quieten his mind, as he did so he rested his head back against the well-worn bottle green upholstery and closed his eyes.

He was hovering somewhere between sleep and consciousness, in a deeply relaxed state he hadn't felt for quite some time, when the doorbell chimed. He

Justice

could see the back panel of Ishan's car on the drive and pulled himself up to answer the door.

"Ishan."

"Tommy."

"Brew?"

"Always."

Once they had discussed a number of work issues and general practicalities, Ishan turned towards him and gently asked.

"How's you then?"

"Yeah. I'm okay thanks, all things considered."

Ishan had called in a few times since Tommy had made his unexpected departure from the office and they had spoken candidly.

"Yeah. About that, any news yet?"

"Not yet."

"You will need to speak to her soon, you know that don't you?"

"Yeah. I know. But it can wait for now."

"I'm sure she will understand you had no choice Tommy, but she does need to hear it from you."

"Yeah I know. The impact this could have on Claire. Her career. That's been the one thing that prevented me from acting sooner Ish."

Ishan looked at him, there was genuine anguish and heartache etched on his tired face. He understood from their recent conversations how Tommy had wrestled with doing the right thing.

"Look all I'm saying is that it's better that she hears it from you. If professional standards contact her first..."

"Yeah. I know." Tommy repeated, avoiding eye contact.

"Look Tommy, she's a clever girl. She'll understand, I'm sure. Something had to be done. Stephenson's not fit

Justice

for the role. The way he's been with Jarvis, you and the Mrs Mazur case but to name a few. You were right to report him. It's not great that Claire will be embroiled and there may well be retrospective implications for her errors on the Mazur thing. But it is what it is, as they say."

Tommy smiled briefly as Ishan used one of the more familiar sayings from his own repertoire.

"Yeah. I know." Tommy said again.

"Look we all know it should have been dealt with properly at the time. It shouldn't have been brushed under the carpet. If Claire comes under fire now, well, that can't be helped can it? You're not responsible for what happens next. You can't protect everyone Tom. You're not everybody's dad, granddad, bloody guardian angel or whatever, you know! You're not responsible for everything. "

"Yeah, I know." he distractedly muttered once more.

Chapter 54

Less than three hours after Ishan's visit Tommy found himself in Wilmslow, driving up an impossibly long and extremely leafy, green approach sitting in the very heart of Cheshire.

As the car turned slightly, simultaneously negotiating a slight brew in the driveway, the innocuous surroundings gave way to the imposing sight of the large closed category prison which housed almost five hundred prisoners at any given time.

Tommy had called ahead and was expected, however, given that he was here to see a category A prisoner; a moniker attributed to only those considered to be the most dangerous of inmates, it took him a while to get through all the necessary security measures.

He was eventually led down a series of bare concrete corridors to a pokey white room that contained only two chairs and a tiny square table, all clearly bolted to

Justice

the floor. Tommy confirmed with the nonplussed officer that he knew the emergency procedures, for the fourth time since he'd arrived, before the prison officer left. He settled himself into the hard plastic and anxiously waited for the door in front of him, at the opposite side of the room, to open.

The cause of the delay became abundantly clear when the door finally opened and the same prison officer entered the small space. He went about the process of securing the prisoner to the table, using a series of chains, all the time giving Tommy the stink eye. It was fair enough he thought, after all he had added to their workload on a Friday evening when it was safe to assume the guards were busy enough. As the officer left he made no attempts to conceal his annoyance at the situation.

"Good evening Detective Marsden. This is a little unorthodox is it not?" she said as a matter of fact.

"Please Mrs McKenzie lets dispense with the formalities shall we? I feel we know each other well enough to be on a first name basis by now, don't you?"

She looked at him in a way that made him feel awkward and uncomfortable. Her stare was intrusive, scrutinising everything about him. It felt as if she could see into his very soul. Tommy held her gaze and maintained his expression.

It was clear to him that despite the environment and the circumstances she still remained stoic and relatively unfazed.

The silence stretched out between them as they quietly weighed up one another until she eventually asked.

"And, to what do I owe the pleasure?"

Tommy figured it was now or never. He had thought about this on the drive over and he had concluded that a direct no-nonsense approach was the only way to go.

Justice

"I want to speak with you about the murder of Edward Grant."

"I gave you a full and comprehensive confession Detective. I'm on remand for Gods sakes." she indicated the room with the limited movement the shackles allowed. "What more pray could there possibly be for us to discuss?"

Tommy hoped she wouldn't notice as he took a sharp breath in preparation. The room was quiet once more until he finally spoke.

"The thing is; I know you didn't kill Mr Grant." He said.

The words hung for a second too long. He would have thought it impossible, but she sat even straighter into the red plastic chair. It was at this point he knew his theory was correct.

"Really, Detective, so why on earth would I have confessed?" She was trying to sound casual.

She held her composure, her eyes never wavering from his. Suddenly Tommy felt the enormity of what he was about to say.

He suddenly had the urge to cough and desperately tried to stave it. His voice softened as he finally said, "Because I know who did."

The air was sucked from the room and Tommy could feel a slight cool dampness on his back, but still Sandy McKenzie appeared unchanged. She remained silent, poised and composed. As she studied him further, in a way that was reminiscent of a beast viewing its latest prey, Tommy now questioned himself. Maybe he was wrong after all, he'd never been much of a gambler, but in a split second he decided that now was the time to 'go all in'.

"There was a stray partial fingerprint on the knife. At the top, just under the handle. On the actual blade itself." he said. "We didn't really bother about it at the time. After all, it was old and you did tell us that you'd got it

Justice

from a car boot." he continued to look deep into her eyes as he elaborated. "The knife could have been handled by hundreds of people in its life time. It could have come from anywhere. And of course we had a complete set of your finger prints." he paused for a moment "In fact your finger prints were perfect," he raised an eyebrow as he continued "perhaps a little too perfect in fact."

When the façade started to crack, it did so with a vengeance. It started with a single silent tear rolling steadily down her left cheek, which she quickly wiped away with her limited movement. But once the flood gates had been breached she sobbed uncontrollably whilst shaking her head and making a howling screeching noise that reminded him of the first time they had met in the relatives room at the local hospital.

He reached into his pocket and pulled out a clean white handkerchief and handed it to her. Later he would recall how even at this stage, sat in desolate surroundings, bound to the desk and clearly hearing such totally devastating news she had simply thanked him for the hankie.

"Why now? Why after all this time?" she sobbed. It seemed she would collapse to the floor if it wasn't for the restraints binding her to the table.

"We'd just discounted the partial print as an anomaly. Just one of those things. Like I say it could have been there for ages, could have belonged to almost anyone. But at a recent dinner party I heard something." He gave a quick tight smile. "The old synapses are not what they used to be. I knew there was something. Something was bothering me, but until today I didn't know what it was.

"I'm sorry." he said. "But justice needs to be done." he watched her reactions as he added "You don't belong here. You didn't do this!"

She had been reduced before his very eyes, but somehow suddenly rallied as she literally begged him to leave her to her fate.

Justice

"A man has died," she spoke quietly now, "someone needs to pay for that. I get that. Justice needs to be done. And I am paying the price for his death, his family's loss. But please hear me out. That bastard got everything he deserved. I will explain everything too you. Just tell me it's not too late. Please!"

Tommy spent the next hour listening to Sandy McKenzie unburden herself.

She explained how a couple of months after her daughter Annabel had killed herself. She became aware of the reality and subsequent consequences of that act, the events her death had set in motion.

"I eventually returned to work," she explained "but it was a thankless endeavour. I could see that colleagues were uncomfortable around me. Suddenly no one seemed to trust me. I'd only been back two days when a young girl came into the resuscitation bay in A&E." She gave a quick, tortured smile before she continued. "I recognise now that it was a hopeless situation...but at the time...well my mind was all over the place, and I just couldn't accept that the girl was dead." she looked into the distance, taking a deep steadying breath. "Anyway, some bright spark decided it would be less stressful, less challenging for me if I were to move to the night shift. Obviously they had never worked nights in a hospital. But there you go." She gave a humourless laugh, as she shifted her weight against the unforgiving plastic.

Tommy was silent throughout.

"I had a couple of weeks off and then went back to work on the night shift. But it was no use. I couldn't do it. I'd become a massive liability." She stopped to dry her eyes once more. "And it wasn't just the big things. I was second guessing myself on practically everything. As a result no one trusted my judgement anymore."

She paused again, but Tommy knew the importance of patience, he wanted her to tell her story in as much detail as possible.

Justice

"Anyway that's how I came to be home on the night of Edward Grants murder. I'd gone to work but was sent home just after midnight to have a 'few days off to pull myself together.' If only it was that bloody simple." She gave him a pathetic micro smile and Tommy couldn't help but feel the rawness of her pain.

"Anyway, I was sat in the garden, you know, near the tree."

He knew exactly where she was indicating, seeing the old oak tree in his mind's eye as she continued.

"So I was smoking, John hates me smoking but...anyway that's when I hear her."

"Kristy, your eldest daughter?" He gently probed.

"Yes."

She looked pale and drawn as she seemed to physically force herself to push on with the description of the events of that terrible night.

"She was covered in blood, it was literally everywhere. She told me what she'd done and why and I just kind of went into overdrive. It was weird really. Given that I couldn't get my shit together with anything else at the time. I just did what I needed to do."

"I wiped the knife handle and rubbed my hand on her bloody clothes before gripping it to leave a clear set of prints on the handle. I than stored it in a paper bag and hid it in the attic in case it was ever needed."

Tommy recalled that as a senior nurse she would know to use a brown paper bag to prevent sample deterioration, that she would be skilled in the art of evidence collection and preservation.

"The clothes?" he asked.

"Burned and the ashes scattered the next day in Worsley Woods."

"Why?"

"Annabel had left a note." She said

Justice

He bristled slightly.

"Oh no, I wasn't lying to you when I said she hadn't. I only found out that night." She clarified

"Kirsty had found the note, hidden in a small jewellery box in her room. That was when she realised he had done the same to her sister as he had done to her." A puff of air which clearly demonstrated her frustration was released before she said. "He deserved everything he got. Every last bloody cut." The look she gave Tommy would stay with him for a very long time as she said quietly "I had no idea. None. What kind of a mother doesn't know what is happening to her own daughters? That low life scumbag had used my daughter and then casually moved along to her younger sister."

Her face hardened now as she met his eyes with a determined stare and simply stated "I had no choice then and I have no choice now. That man has destroyed enough of my life. I have lost one daughter because of his vile depraved actions and I won't lose another. I won't see Kirsty's life ruined by this. She has a chance to put this behind her...To have a happy life."

He was dumbfounded for a moment. Like most people he'd heard anecdotes of mothers going to extra ordinary lengths to protect their children.

"But this? This is not right." He said indicating the room.

Her resolve was restored and once again she was two steps ahead of him.

"Detective. You have nothing against my daughter. Not one scrap of evidence. I will testify, if asked, that I lied about the provenance of the knife, that it wasn't a car boot find, but a family heirloom. My grandfathers, from the war, it had been in my attic for a number of years. Kirsty could have touched it at any point in its history." She was resolute and steadfast as she ploughed on. "You have no clothes worn and no evidence of any credible motive, outside what I have told you. I have confessed and there is absolutely no reasonable doubt that I did not do this."

Justice

She was right of course.

"I am begging you Detective, please just leave this alone. Have you never loved someone so much that you would do anything for them? I know this is not right, but I am happy to do the time, to pay the dept. I'm happy to pervert the course of justice. I'm happy to break the law in favour of what I know to be right. Please leave me be Detective!"

She gave him a sad smile, her wet eyes glistening in the harsh lights again as she said "After all, don't you know, everyone in here is innocent."

Chapter 55

Climbing into his car in the shadow of the colossal prison he felt drained. He had known something was bothering him for a while and he now knew what it was. He instinctively rubbed his right hand as he recalled now, how as a child his Grandfather had only raised his voice at him once, as far as he could remember, that had been when he had reached for a hot soldering iron in their little shed. His small hand had struggled with the bulk of the insulated handle and his little finger was badly burned as a result. When at the dinner party Josie had talked of Emmett as a boy, his mischievous ways and how she struggled with disciplining him; she had set his mind off wandering. And it was only when Ishan had been so blunt with him, stating that he couldn't protect everyone, in particular that he couldn't protect Claire from what might happen as a result of his complaint to professional standards about Stephenson, that he wasn't the Granddad in the situation that it all just slid into focus.

Justice

Would he have joined the dots sooner if he hadn't been so busy he wondered, he would never know. But as he drove down the long, now dark driveway, he also knew it was all academic. Yes, he knew the truth. He knew that young Annabel had taken her own life. He knew that Edward Grant had preyed on at least two innocent young girls during his life and of course he knew that Sandy McKenzie was innocent of his murder. He rubbed his eyes and pinched the bridge of his nose as he waited to join a long stream of traffic at a main junction, questioning if he was in fact better off before he knew.

Epilogue

Two months later

"Well, this is a nice surprise. How are you Detective?" She asked as the prison guard banged the door closed.

"I'm well Sandy. And you?"

"Yeah. I'm good thanks. I'm doing okay." She gave a wide smile as she said "Actually, I don't want to brag or anything, but I'm the prison wings favoured 'unofficial nurse'." She did the air quotes with her fingers for emphasis. "I'm the first port of call for medical advice on lumps, bumps and minor ailments; not just for the inmates either!" Her smile continued and he realised that she looked more relaxed today than at any other time that they had met.

"I heard about the sentencing and-"

"A walk in the park Detective. I have no regrets." She looked him in the eye as she said a heartfelt thank you.

They were quiet for a beat before he told her that he had seen the house was up for sale.

"That's right, John and Kirsty have moved away. Turns out he was stronger than I gave him credit for in the end." There was a hint of anger or was it remorse in her words.

The tiny room was still once more before she said "I am so grateful to you for leaving things alone Tommy, but you never told me why."

Of course he had known that one day she would ask this question. He'd rehearsed an answer about the lack of evidence, that there was no legitimate reason to open up the case again etcetera, and of course that was all true. But instead he spoke the actual truth. His voice was low and tinged with sadness as he explained "When you spoke of unconditional love. About doing anything necessary for someone you care for, even breaking the law...Well that kind of resonated with me personally." He knew he had said too much as she stared at him for a few seconds before he pressed the button on the wall, summoning the guard. He only stopped to say goodbye and to wish her good luck for the future.

Once alone in the car, he wept uncontrollably as he remembered Cathy's final hours. How he had done what needed to be done to end her pain, her suffering. He'd done it because he loved her so very deeply. She was his everything.

<u>Coming soon!</u>

If you have enjoyed Justice, look out for Betrayal, which is the next book in the Detective Inspector Thomas Marsden series.

When a child suddenly disappears the team are under extreme pressure to find her as quickly as possible. Tommy finds himself haunted by the shadows of his past, as he races against the clock to prevent history repeating itself.

Printed in Great Britain
by Amazon